T]

THE GLASS HOUSE

by

V. J. Banis

Writing as "Jan Alexander"

The Borgo Press
An Imprint of Wildside Press

MMVII

Copyright © 1972, 2007 by V. J. Banis

All rights reserved.
No part of this book may be reproduced in any form
without the expressed written consent of the author and
publisher. Printed in the United States of America

SECOND EDITION

PROLOGUE

A young woman stood alone in a darkened room. A faint glow of light came from the open window near where she stood; it was sufficient illumination to make her cheeks glisten where the tears had been trickling across them. Another tear spilled from the corner of her eye just then, only one, and slid downward over her cheek, slowly at first, and then with more confidence, disappearing at the chin line; it left still another glistening trail.

She made no sound. Her crying was silent, even reluctant. She had been taught not to cry. Although the room was shabby and her dress several times mended, she had the demeanor usually associated with wealth and breeding.

A door opened behind her. Harsh yellow light, the kind thrown by a naked bulb, tumbled into the room in a distorted rectangle.

"Mademoiselle?"

She did not turn until she had brushed away the most recent tear and was certain she could speak without any difficulty.

In fact, there was no need for words. The young boy at the door was French, and eyed her with Gaelic solemnity. The priest in the next room was French too, French Canadian. She had requested that when she made the call, and no one had questioned it. Few people cared to challenge the whims of the dying; perhaps they knew that they too would want succor when the time came.

Inwardly she felt the reluctance that is natural when one must approach death, but there was no hesitation in her manner. She came past the boy, out of the room. Because he looked so frightened, she thought that he had not served in this capacity before, and she put her hand gently and briefly upon his shoulder to reassure him. He rewarded her with a quick smile.

The priest stood at the door of the room across the hall. He took her hand and patted it, prepared to offer her sympathy or words of courage if she needed them. She did not show that she needed either, though, and he stepped aside to let her come into the room.

It was a room that tried to look less austere than it was. A picture of the Virgin, clipped long ago from some forgotten magazine and framed in a dime-store frame gave a spot of color to one wall, and on the dresser across the room stood a very old arrangement of beaded flowers. But they did not hide the hideous condition of the wall plaster or the fact that the dresser had a stack of books where one leg ought to be.

The priest had noted these things. He was an observant man who liked to collect details about the many people whose lives touched his. He knew that this young girl, with her pale china doll's face, and her mother, who lay dying on the sagging bed, were very poor. But he knew too that they had not always been this poor. They wore their poverty like a temporary thing to which they had never quite become accustomed. He wondered, quite irrelevantly under the circumstances, what had happened to the wealth they had once possessed.

The girl had gone straight to the bed, and had taken her mother's limp hand in her own. She leaned over the bed, listening to something that her mother was trying to say. She made a reply, but her voice was only a murmur to the priest's ears.

He stepped out of the room and pulled the door gently closed. Behind him the little altar boy shifted his weight cautiously from one foot to the other.

Harrod. That was the name the young lady had given him. He had meant to address her by name a moment before, but the name had slipped his mind. He said it again, to establish it more firmly in his mind, so that he could use it later. He was a kindly man. He did not like people to be nameless at times such as these.

The bedroom was lighted by candles that burned

steadily because there was no movement of the close air. They, or perhaps the moment that was swiftly approaching, gave a yellowish pallor to the face of the woman on the bed. Her eyes were feverish, her cheeks sunken. Her breath was a rattle in her throat.

Only the strength of a great passion permitted her to linger on for these few moments. She knew she was going to die. She had no fear of that. She was leaving behind a thousand griefs and agonies, and only one happiness: the daughter leaning over her now.

But she could not go until she had settled this one thing. She had not even been able to confess properly because her old hatred had kept intruding, and with it the fear that she might not have time to get this straight with her daughter.

Now, however, the moment eluded her. With so little time, her mind seemed to drift away from the one thing that mattered. In her thoughts she was going back. She heard the piping and the singing of old. She had remembered it often enough; but this was not the same as remembering. This was as if she had actually gone back, and for a brief instant she was home. She breathed the sea air, and laughed, and was happy again. The years of hurt and hatred and bitterness moved away, into the shadows. A young man called her name. She thrilled in her breast because she knew that she was lovely and a handsome young man loved her.

A tear fell upon her face. It was like a knocking

that brings you from daydreams back to the present moment. Her eyes flew open for the last time.

"Margaree," she whispered hoarsely. She could no longer distinguish her daughter's face, but she felt her presence, and was sure she was somewhere near.

"I'm here," the familiar voice said.

"Promise me." The piping was back, louder. It seemed to be calling her, and her body responded. She felt lighter. The pain was gone, and her feet wanted to dance.

"Promise me. I want revenge. I want Stornoway, for you. You must get it back."

Her feet would hardly be still. The fete was beginning, and she was eager to be off and in the arms of her man. But this had to be settled.

"I want revenge on the Harrods," she gasped. "I want Stornoway."

Margaree could not quite keep back a sob. She knew the old stories. She knew of her mother's hatred and resentment. But she had never felt them before. They had seemed curious things to her, but they were not hers to share with her mother. They belonged to a past she did not know, that was only a mystery to her.

Now, though, she was in the presence of the greatest of all mysteries; for a moment she stood on the threshold of death and saw that what had seemed a chasm was only a single step. From some source within her that she had not even known existed rose a bitterness, even a hate, to answer her mother's. It leaped up within the agony of her grief, and took hold of her aching heart.

"I promise," she whispered.

Her mother did not hear her, though. She had gone dancing.

Hundreds of miles away, a man stirred in his sleep. His wife, who did not share his room but had come to look in on him, went to his bedside and put a hand on his forehead, as if the images of his dreams might thus be transmitted through her fingertips to her own brain.

He opened his eyes. The sadness lingering in them fled at sight of her. He was quite mad, but with her he was like a docile child.

"Antoinette," he said. "I was frightened. I had a dream about dying."

"It's all right," she said, patting his head. "I'm here. I want you to go back to sleep." It was a command, delivered in a soft voice, but a command nonetheless. He closed his eyes and drifted obediently back to sleep. Antoinette was here. There was nothing to be afraid of, not even death himself. Even he would not dare stand up to Antoinette.

CHAPTER 1

It was nearly a year later that the same Margaree walked along a street in Boston. It had been a lonely year for her. She and her mother had been very close, perhaps all the more so because of the meanness of their existence, and it had been a long time before she could think of her mother without feeling as if a sharp instrument had been thrust into her heart.

She had not forgotten her promise. In fact, it occupied her thoughts just now, so completely so that she stepped from a curb into the street without giving any thought to the light.

Tires squealed on pavement, and a car came to a stop ominously close to her. A man leaned out the window, looking very angry.

"Hey," he said in a belligerent voice. But he

stopped because she had turned toward him, her eyes a little frightened, her lips parted slightly. Something about her arrested him. It was not merely that she was pretty. She was, but no more so than many other girls. It was something about the frightened look she wore; it made her look younger than her twenty-three years. She had a vulnerable quality that aroused the protective instincts in the male breast. She had composure, to be sure; she had recovered almost at once from her fright. But her self-possession was only superficial. Beneath it you saw at once that she had a timid quality. That she wanted to be loved, to be helped, and sheltered, and a man's instincts rose to the call.

"You'd better be more careful, Miss," he said in a much quieter voice. And because she still looked a little uncertain, he smiled and motioned her to cross in front of his car. He watched her go along the street until the car behind him sounded its horn impatiently, and he had to drive on.

She came to the marquee of a hotel, and hesitated outside the thick glass doors. This was her destination; at least, it was her immediate destination. Her final destination was still a long way off, far to the north.

She hesitated on the sidewalk, until a man in a gaudy uniform asked, "Can I help you, miss?"

"No, thank you," she said quickly, and went in before he could question her further.

Once inside, her feet carried her to the elevator. There was no need to stop at the desk. She knew the number of the suite. She was expected at three, and it was almost exactly that now.

No, she corrected herself as the elevator carried her swiftly and silently upward, she was not expected. M. Butler was expected at 3 P.M. Nor was there any doubt in her mind that the Harrods thought M. Butler was a man. Even the very letter she carried in her purse, confiming this appointment, began: *Dear Mr. Butler . . .*

The elevator stopped, and the doors slid open. Still moving by impulse, she stepped out and a moment later the elevator had glided on, leaving her to stand alone in the garish, deeply carpeted hall.

She walked toward the end of the wall, reading the numbers on the doors. She came to the door marked 614, and paused outside it.

She had a moment of panic. It was no use, she thought, she could not carry it off. It was one thing to make a promise at her mother's deathbed. It was another to set out on a journey to revenge.

Not revenge, she quickly corrected herself. Justice, that was what she was seeking. She wanted only what had rightly been her mother's; and not for her own sake, either. Once she had claimed it in her mother's name, she would happily go away. She simply wanted to see right done.

But wanting was one thing, getting was another. She was too weak a person for what she had started out to do. An opportunity had presented itself and, on a tide of emotion, she had seized it, not realizing until afterward that it required more than she had to give. It required a boldness she simply did not possess, and wits quicker than hers, to carry off pretense such as she had begun.

It was useless. She had made a foolish mistake in using her mother's maiden name to set up this appointment, in even thinking she could do what she had planned to do. She must go away, now, at once. She would call them later, from that tiny little room she had rented this morning, and tell them she had deceived them and that M. Butler was not a man, but a woman. They would be annoyed, of course, and they would explain that they did indeed want a man. That would end it.

And wouldn't that be better after all? It was all well and good to call her motive justice, and not revenge. But whatever it was called, she had seen what it had done to her mother, had watched it year in and year out turn her mother into a woman sick and old before her time. Wasn't it just as well to let it lie, be done with it once and for all? Stornoway meant nothing to her. It was a name, a distant place.

She came to the very verge of turning about and making her way back to the elevator. In another moment, she would have done so, and her entire life would have been different.

But in that moment during which she hesitated, the door before which she stood opened. She had been so absorbed in her thoughts that she had not noticed the voices beyond the door, growing louder and louder as conversation became argument. Now, suddenly, the door flew open, and a man appeared. He was in the act of leaving the room in a rather violent manner. But she was in his path, making him stop short.

His angry eyes raked over her. "What do you want?" he demanded rudely.

"I . . ." she faltered. His manner was intimidating, virtually overpowering. There was a wildness about him that made her suddenly shy so that for a moment she could do nothing but stare open-mouthed at him.

He was not handsome in the ordinary sense of the word. But the power of his presence was considerable. His eyes flashed, seeming to see everything at once. His hair was an unruly tangle of dark curls. He wore a shaggy jacket and loose, worn trousers. He looked very out of place amid the hotel's loud opulence.

That thought finally brought her back to her senses. She had made a mistake of some sort; she must have come to the wrong door after all. This rough hewn creature before her was certainly not Marc Harrod, who had written such neat, polished letters to her regarding the job. The Harrods might live by the sea, but they were not fishermen, which was exactly what this man looked to be.

"Well?" he said with ill-concealed impatience.

"I'm afraid I've made a mistake," she said, regaining a little of her composure. "I was looking for the Harrod suite."

"You've made no mistake," he said. "This is the Harrod suite. Who are you?"

A moment before she had wanted to turn and run like a scared rabbit. But his persistent rudeness touched some hidden switch within her, fanned a spark of pride that her mother had long kept alive. She pulled her shoulders back, and her chin up.

"I'm Margaree Butler," she said coolly. "I have an appointment with Mr. Marc Harrod. Are you he?"

"I am Mr. Harrod," a voice said from within the room.

She had been aware that others were in the room, but she had been unable to take her eyes off the man before her long enough to observe them. Now he stepped aside, giving her a look that was more curious than angry.

She took his movement to be an invitation of sorts, and stepped into the room before anyone had the opportunity to forbid her entrance.

The man who had identified himself as Marc Harrod was just inside the room, so that she almost ran into him coming in. He was what she had been expecting, although a little more handsome than she had anticipated. His was a sleek, elegant handsomeness though, not at all like the raw power of the man who had first greeted her.

"I'm Margaree Butler," she said again, addressing him directly this time. "I wrote about the tutoring position."

"Then I'm afraid you have made a mistake," he said, looking only slightly discomposed. "We wanted a man for the job." His eyes added, pointedly, that they had been expecting her to be one.

"I know," she said bluntly.

Her honesty seemed to leave him at something of a loss. After a moment he said, "Perhaps you can offer an explanation."

"There's really very little to explain," she said. "I needed employment. I heard about this opening, and I applied for the job." She did not tell of the effort she had put forth to find a way to get close to the family, or how jubilant she had been when fate had provided the chance in the form of a tutoring job.

"You applied as a man," he said, making an accusation of it.

"I never said that I was, and you never asked," she replied.

He seemed less angry, and even a bit amused. "You have spunk," he said. "But I'm afraid I shall have to disappoint you after all. We did want . . ."

"Marc." A woman's voice interrupted him. It was a crisp, authoritative voice, one accustomed to giving commands, and having them obeyed. Marc Harrod plainly was accustomed to obeying. He snapped about at once.

Margaree turned too. She had been unaware of another presence in the room, so intent had she been on explaining herself to Marc.

The woman had placed herself in a large, uncomfortable-looking chair almost in the corner, so that she could observe without being noticed. She sat in it stiffly; the effect was not unlike that of a queen upon a throne.

Her appearance added to that effect. She was a handsome woman, beautiful, but in an icy cold way. She was closer to fifty than to forty, but her jet black hair had ignored any suggestion of graying. Her eyes were brown, but so dark that they too appeared to be black, and this gave her frank gaze a penetrating quality. There were no laugh lines about her mouth. Looking at her, you had the impression she was not in the corner of the room at all, but in its center.

Margaree knew of course who she was. She had not expected to meet her yet, here in this hotel. But she would have known her anywhere. She had heard of this woman from her early childhood; indeed, they had looked upon each other before, in her earliest childhood, but that was too long ago for Margaree to remember. What she did remember were her mother's stories of this woman's beauty, beauty that had given her power over men's minds and their natural instincts, so that she could twist them to her own selfish purposes.

The woman held a silver-handled walking stick before her, her hands resting atop its handle. She held it as a monarch might hold a scepter, and now she tapped once, sharply, on the floor.

"I want to talk to this girl," she said. It was a command. The entire pattern of the world might hinge upon those words "I want."

Certainly to Marc Harrod that was true. His manner was so servile that Margaree half-expected him to bow.

"My mother," he said, "Mrs. Harrod. Miss Butler. I've forgotten what the M was for."

Before Margaree could supply it, Mrs. Harrod said, "Margaree. How do you do."

Margaree nearly bowed herself, and immediately resented the impulse. It was not difficult to understand how Antoinette Harrod had managed to take over a family and fortune. Just now she managed, with no pause at all, to take over the scene at hand.

"My sons, to whom you haven't been properly introduced," Mrs. Harrod said. "Marc Harrod, and Jean Copley." She indicated with a flick of her eyes the man who had first opened the door of the suite.

Margaree was surprised to lear that Jean was Antoinette Harrod's son also. Yet she shouldn't have been, she thought as she acknowledged the introduction. She had known that there was another son by a previous marriage. And now that she saw him again, she saw that he looked a great deal like his mother. The eyes especially were alike; although his lacked the coldness of hers, they were equally striking, and equally penetrating. Even his powerful presence was like hers, although again without quite that sense of cruel selfishness. You had the feeling that he too wanted to rule, but only his own private world and life.

Right now that desire seemed to be in conflict with Mrs. Harrod's.

"I'm going," he said. He acknowledged his introduction to Margaree with a curt nod, and strode purposefully toward the door.

"You may go," Antoinette Harrod said after him, as if giving him imperial leave.

His back stiffened slightly, and he paused. There was no doubt that he resented her authoritative manner, and for a moment he seemed unable to decide whether to stay or to go. But she had created a situation in which to do either was an acquiescence to her wishes. He went after all, the door crashing shut after him.

Mrs. Harrod seemed not to notice the rudeness of his departure. Having dismissed him, she had been studying Margaree.

"I want to ask you some questions," she said. She did not wait for permission, but asked, "Where are you from?"

"Carver, Massachusetts," Margaree said. She stood with her feet together, hands clasped primly before her. She felt as if she were back at school, and giving an oral recitation.

"Have you always lived there?"

"As long as I can remember." It was more or less the truth. What she knew of the years before Carver, she knew mostly secondhand.

"And I suppose your family is still there?" Antoinette Harrod's keen eyes seemed to grow darker still.

"I have no family," Margaree said. Even now, the statement gave her a little stab of pain. She wondered what this cold woman before her would say if she replied, "You are my family." She felt certain she would receive no openarmed welcome. Instead she said, "My mother died a year ago."

"And your father?"

"When I was very young."

The older woman seemed to digest this information for a moment. Margaree knew they were on treacherous ground. Lying was a difficult business for her. Each time she had to use the name Butler, her tongue stumbled on it. She had made up her mind before coming to tell as much of the truth as she possibly could. It never occurred to her that her honesty was a moral thing. She told the truth because it was quite difficult for her to lie.

Again she suffered self-doubt. How could she hope to deceive anyone, let alone this clever woman before her? She was a fool to have thought she could pit herself against this creature who had outwitted so many others.

"I hope you are not thinking that the job should be an act of charity," Margaree said impulsively. "I have other interviews already arranged, and some of them are for local jobs. Perhaps you're right, perhaps you should have a man for your job . . ."

"I think I'm the best judge of that," Mrs. Harrod said, effectively ending her speech. "I think you will do quite well for what we had in mind. Marc will arrange all of the details with you."

There was no question as to whether Margaree would accept the job, or the salary offered, or any such thing. She was not to be permitted any questions or reservations. She had been told virtually nothing about the job. Antoinette Harrod had made up her mind, and so the matter was settled, as quickly and as finally as that.

For a very brief moment, Margaree hesitated. She had been again on the verge of retreating. The pendulum of uncertainty had carried her back from the threshold of her venture, had given her a last chance to forget this entire business, to free herself from the bitter past, and begin instead her own life.

But Antoinette Harrod had taken that decision from her, and settled the question. She had reached out and seized the pendulum, and brought it to rest where it best suited her. And so, Margaree thought, it shall be; and she felt a sense of relief that it was decided, for better or for worse.

"Thank you," she said aloud, and at Marc's suggestion she went with him into an adjoining room to discuss the salary, and make arrangements for transportation to the Harrod home.

"It's a good distance from here," he said. "On the isle of Cape Breton, off the Nova Scotia coast. Do you know where that is?"

"I've heard of it," she said simply, which was quite an understatement.

Antoinette Harrod forbade her fingers to drum on the silver handle of her walking stick. It gave an impression of uncertainty, and she never gave that impression. She closed her eyes, turning her sight inward, and thought very hard about the young girl with whom she had just spoken. There had been no charity in giving the girl the job. She was not much inclined toward charity. She did not like parting with what was hers, and she did not much care if other people thought her ungenerous.

She was a pretty girl, that one. Antoinette conjured up an image of her face. It was the face of some one who had a secret. Whether that secret bade well or ill for her, she could not yet say, but she knew that it concerned her. The girl's beauty was psychological, not plastic, and the smile that toyed with the corners of her mouth when she was thinking was too subtle to be sweet.

She was the Gioconda in a mended yellow dress.

CHAPTER 2

When you travel north from Boston and get beyond that cluttered city, you find yourself in the New England of a century ago, a New England of forested mountains and serene villages. Long before you reach the Canadian border, you begin to encounter a people who are shorter, darker of skin, and seemingly more vivacious; and if you ask for directions, they may be given in French.

Of course Marc Harrod had no need to ask directions.

"As early as 1500, maybe even earlier," he explained as he drove, "French fishermen were crossing the Atlantic to fish in the coastal waters here."

Margaree was beside him in the front seat. The car was a Rolls-Royce. She had seen one once when she had been a small girl; her mother had pointed at it and said, "If there were any justice, you'd be riding in a car like that." And now she was, so perhaps there would be justice, after all.

Antoinette Harrod sat in the rear. There was a glass partition between the two seats, but it was rolled down now. Despite this fact, she seemed uninterested in, perhaps unaware of, the conversation in the front seat. She watched the scenes gliding by outside the window, but not as if they much excited her enthusiasm.

Jean Copley was not with them. No explanation had been offered for his absence, and Margaree had hardly thought it right that she should ask. She did not know why she had felt vaguely disappointed to see that he was not in the car.

"The first attempts to establish colonies didn't go very well." Marc went on: "And for a time the fishermen had the place rather to themselves. But in the late 1500s furs became fashionable. The entire Canadian area was rich in furs, and trading became a big industry. Adventurous Frenchmen took to the forests as *coureurs de bois*—woods runners.

"There were so few women in those early French colonies that the royal government took to importing shiploads of them."

"The *filles du roi*," Margaree said, forgetting that she ought to be ignorant of those things.

He seemed pleased, however, that she knew a little of the local history, and did not seem to question why it should have interested her. She thought it would please him less if he knew why.

"Yes," he said, "the king's girls. They came from orphanages, peasant families, even prisons. They got a dowry of provisions and household goods. If they accumulated ten living children, they earned a royal pension, with a bonus for two more. Most of the French Canadians are descendants of the king's girls."

They had come up through Maine to Saint John on the Bay of Fundy.

"The Maritime Provinces fared better as colonies," Marc continued while they waited for the ferry. "The French established a colony in the Annapolis Valley across the bay. It became Acadia, prospered in its forgotten corner of the world, and was memorialized in Longfellow's poem, *Evangeline*."

The ferry took them across to Digby. The English name of that town gave evidence that France was only a part of the history of the region. Nova Scotia had first belonged to France, who had built powerful fortresses in an attempt to check the expansion of the aggressive English colonies. But in the mid-eighteenth century the forts were taken by the British, and the French settlers, the Acadians, were expelled and their lands given to British and New England immigrants.

After the American War of Revolution, many New Englanders who had been loyal to the crown immigrated to the area, joining with Scots and Germans. Some of the Acadians returned, along with other French Canadians. From this mixture of diversified elements had come the people of Nova Scotia.

The diversity was apparent along the way. It was like traveling through a variety of countries in a short span of time. Lunenberg, through which they passed, was as German as Halifax was British, and Antigonish, the last town on the mainland, had a distinctly Scottish flavor.

But all of this was only a prelude to their destination, Cape Breton. From her earliest childhood she had heard of that isle. Her mother's stories had centered on that one remote locale, that tiny island off the Nova Scotian mainland. This was her mother's beloved homeland; everything here was more beautiful; the storms were fiercer, the people nicer, the fish bigger.

It seemed to have taken far too long for her to come here. She approached it now with a mixed feeling of excited anticipation and skepticism; surely nothing could be as grand as this place had been described to her.

Cape Breton's history was as mixed as that of the other provinces. Fishermen from all over the world —from France, England, Spain, Portugal—had visited here and gathered the treasures of the sea. But the island belonged perhaps most of all to the Scottish. The Reverend Norman MacLeod, adventurer and clergyman, unhappy with the mainland of

Nova Scotia in 1817, had sailed away; a storm had forced him and his followers to the island. They found the rugged land similar to their homeland and they stayed to found settlements with such names as Loch Lomond, Strathlorne, and Inverness.

The French and English fought for the possession of the island, as they did for the rest of Nova Scotia, and each of them owned it from time to time. In 1621 King James I presented a royal charter and a coat of arms to a Scottish gentleman, Sir William Alexander, and Acadia was renamed Nova Scotia, or New Scotland. In 1713 the Treaty of Utrecht gave Nova Scotia to Great Britain, but Cape Breton, or Ile Royale as it was known, remained French and later Canadian.

She knew all the details of the history. For bedtime stories her mother had regaled her with legends of the isle, stories about the giant, Angus McAskill, called the strongest man in the world, and Murdock Morrison, the Gaelic bard of Cape Breton, who had a golden tongue.

Late in the afternoon they approached the Causeway, called the road to the isle, that spanned the seventeen-mile-long "Gut of Canso" to join the island to the mainland.

Margaree felt a quickening of her pulse. They were on the island now. She knew before he turned, which roads Marc would take. They went north and east, toward Baddeck. Here Alexander Graham Bell had kept his summer home, with the musical name Beinn Bhreagh, which translated to beautiful hill. Nor was it hard to see how the place had gotten its name.

They circled the Bras d'Or lakes—the arms of gold.

"This is the Margaree Valley," Marc said as they came out of the village of Baddeck. "Spelled just like your name, as a matter of fact. Quite a coincidence, now that you think of it."

She thought that Mrs. Harrod, in the rear seat, sat forward a little at that comment, and to change the subject, she said quickly, "Oh, what a frightening road."

It was; it twisted sharply upward. Some of the curves were hair raising, and conversation dwindled for a time as Marc concentrated on his driving. Margaree was content to sit and watch, and anticipate what was to come.

After Ingonish the trail wound up toward Cape Smoky, called that because of the fleecy mist that half-obscured it. Along this stretch were series of small fishing villages—Wreck Cove, Indian Brook, Skir Dhu, which meant black rock in Gaellic, and Saint Anne's, named for Queen Anne of Austria.

At last they were approaching Stornoway. She knew, even before Marc said, "Almost there. You'll be able to see it soon."

She came close to telling him that she had been seeing it for years, as her mother had described it. In her mind was fixed a picture of it, and the details that her mother had not supplied had been provided by her imagination. For a moment she closed her eyes and studied the picture as she had it fixed in her memory. She saw pale walls and towers lifting above black cliffs.

She opened her eyes and saw the incredible reality of it in the distance.

It was like what she had pictured, and yet altogether different. The walls and towers were gray and time-pocked, with heavy rooftops. It was a majestic huddle of shabby masonry under a gray sky. No longer was it something only to savor in her imagination. It was real. People—her ancestors—had lived here for hundreds of years, and still did live in it. Her mother had known this place; she had traveled toward it just like this, and surely with the same sense of coming home.

The road curved and the house disappeared. They were driving through one of the little fishing villages. Another time she would have been enchanted by the town, but now she was impatient. She watched steadily out the windows of the car for another glimpse. She did not even notice the close way in which the woman in the back seat was watching her.

Some people in the street turned to look at the car. Margaree saw peasant faces, curious eyes. A large, shaggy dog began to bark and ran after the car until it had well outdistanced him.

At the opposite edge of the town one road turned sharply to the west. They went by it. The car went straight up another, very steep drive. At the top Marc steered to the left, into an old paved courtyard.

She was here, at Stornoway, actually within the walls. All about her the ancient stones rose to meet the cold sky. With the engine turned off, they were surrounded by a silence that only added to the sense of timelessness. It was an intrusion when Marc opened the door on his side noisely, and she had to do the same.

Margaree got out of the car in a fog. She felt as if her feet had walked over these hard stones before. Of course she had been a mere baby when she had been here then. But she had been here a hundred times since in spirit, if not in fact. It was in her blood. The gray walls called greeting to her, and something within her answered.

Yes, she was home. All her fears and doubts notwithstanding, she had made, or been guided to, the right decision. This was where she belonged. She would never leave here again. She would keep the promise she had made to her mother.

CHAPTER 3

Antoinette Harrod had scarcely seen the Cape Breton landscapes rushing by the windows of the car. Her mind had been crowded with other scenes.

She knew who the girl in the front seat was; she was certain of it. She had guessed at the first, but since then she had become convinced. The Butler name; the first name with its distorted spelling; where else but in Cape Breton did they spell it like that; more than anything else, the excited way in which the child devoured each new vista, as if she were coming to visit the magical kingdoms of her childhood fairy tales.

She was sure this was Julie Butler's daughter.

But what was she doing here, hiding behind her mother's maiden name? What did she want?

Antoinette smiled at her own faint reflection in

the window glass. Nonsense. It was obvious what she wanted. But what did she know that made her think she could get it? It was this question that had made her, even suspecting the girl's real identity, give Margaree the tutoring job. It would be easiest to keep an eye on her if she were close at hand; and especially if she thought no one suspected who she really was.

She leaned back against the plush upholstery of the car. She had thought she was through with all that. She had gotten rid of them once, and so many years had passed since, that she had written finish to it in her mind. But there was still that one matter never resolved; that could be troublesome, if someone started meddling.

She sighed, and let her thoughts drift back, back to that other time. She thought of the first time she had seen Stornoway. She had known at once that she must have it for her own—not to share, but hers to rule. She had known from the first that nothing would prevent that; nothing could, when once she had made her mind up. She had come as a widow, although still a young woman, with a son, young Jean. She had stayed as a bride and next in line for the throne; if, that is, one discounted her husband, Yves.

Her thoughts drifted to Josh Harrod. The old man. He had been master of the house then, and of the Harrod fortune. She smiled. She had rather liked him, although she would never have let him see that. He had the backbone to stand up to her.

She liked that in a man. It gave her a sense of challenge.

Yves had never had any spine. All in all, he was detestable. But never mine; he had married her anyway, and given her Stornoway, because he was the oldest son.

She had often wished she had met the other son, Waldo. He had been the old man's favorite, and from everything she had heard, he must have been a man of some strength. She had no doubt that she could have persuaded him to marry her. Of course then it would have been necessary to get rid of Yves somehow, so that Waldo could inherit. But she had often let her thoughts ramble through these fantasies, and she had in mind several ways she could have done it. She had always been clever.

Waldo had been married, and dead, however, before she had come into the picture. He had suffered a drowning accident, and left behind his wife, Julie, and her soon to be born daughter.

If only she had known about the accident. But she hadn't, and stupid Yves, wanting so desperately to marry and win some little portion of his father's favor, hadn't told her. So they married at the most distasteful of times, when Yves ought to have been mourning his brother. That had put the old man against her. He had taken the widow and newlyborn granddaughter under his wing, and nothing she could do served to usurp that place.

Still, she had always known that fate somehow would bend to her will.

"It's so lucky," she had said to Yves one day, "that there are no relatives to confuse the inheritance."

"What a strange thing to say," he had replied. "There's all sorts of relatives. Julie and Margaree, to name just two."

She had laughed. "Oh, I mean relatives who could do anything about the money."

He had asked her later, a little sadly, "Did you only marry me for the money, then?"

"That," she said frankly, "and the house."

Fate had come close to cheating her. She hadn't known about the other will. No one had ever said a thing about it until the old man, taking sick rather suddenly, had died. Then that insipid daughter-in-law had raised a hue and a cry about a new will, giving her Stornoway in trust for Margaree, until Margaree came of age.

In the end, though, victory had been hers. The new will was not to be found. The old man had hidden it, and had not gotten around to telling where it was hidden. Antoinette never doubted for a moment that there was a will. In retrospect, she could see that the signs had pointed that way. But a lost will was, from her point of view, a nonexistent will. The old will made Yves, as the oldest son, the heir. That, in effect, gave her Stornoway and made her mistress of the estate.

Yves had made some feeble objections, of course, when she had thrown Julie and her wretched child out of the house. But at the best of times he was no match for her temper. He had always taken to drugs, opium was the least of them, and Heaven alone knew what else. She had encouraged it, because it meant he left her alone. The emotional shock of his father's death, and her encouragement, had driven him deeper and deeper into his drug-induced dream world that had eventually become, for him, a nightmare. The time had come when she had had to buy his drugs for him, dealing with all sorts of unsavory people. And finally the time had come when she stopped buying, because it no longer mattered. His dreams and his nightmares were the same, whether she pandered to his addictions or not. Yves had gone mad.

She felt neither guilt nor remorse. She cared for him at Stornoway, because she thought it would not have been right to send him to some asylum. And, of course, it meant that she was absolute mistress of Stornoway, and had her way in everything, as she had known all along she would eventually anyway. Julie and her baby had been sent away, never to come back. Stornoway was hers. Yves was out of the picture for all practical purposes. It was all settled. Or should have been.

"Mother."

She started. She had closed her eyes without realizing it. She found Marc's eyes on her in the mirror of the car.

"We're almost there," he said.

"I am aware of it," she said crossly. She pulled her shoulders back and clenched her walking stick tightly.

And now this. This girl gawking out the window, giving herself away at every look. In a moment she would be squealing. She was the picture of her mother; pretty, but too soft. She would be easy to break, as her mother had been broken.

Unless she knew something about the will. Surely, after all these years it would remain lost.

What had brought her back here? The question gnawed at Antoinette.

They were there, at Stornoway. Marc came back to help her out of the car. Margaree got out herself —like a peasant. Antoinette watched her staring about with awe. She saw her son watching the girl too. Yes, there was something to be remembered and used later. Marc liked a pretty face, and the girl had one. And Marc was a good-looking boy; he would be able to charm her, and get the truth out of her, if it came to that.

Antoinette smiled and walked regally toward the house. This would come to nothing. She would see to that. But first she would keep a sharp eye out, to determine just what, if anything, this intruder knew.

Servants were coming out of the house. A middle-aged man in black was discussing baggage with Marc. A plump woman in a frilly dress came to stand in the doorway. She did not look frightfully happy to see them.

Margaree stood resolutely on the stone paving, looking about her. In her mind she was willing roots down, determining that she would stay. Now that she had come at last to Stornoway, she meant to cling like a barnacle.

At the moment, though, no one was trying to dislodge her. On the contrary, Marc was hurrying her inside when she would have liked to linger where she was for a time, savoring each new sight.

"This way," he said, motioning at her in a commanding way. She resented it momentarily, until she reminded herself that she was a servant—in their eyes. She came with him into a large echoing gloominess, with people in it.

It was a large, cold, bare hall, slightly furnished, but not so that it was made to look particularly hospitable. The small square tiles of the floor had been worn to a stone color by years of treading feet, but in the corners she could still distinguish a bright floral glaze that her mother had described to her. The walls were wood paneled; the wood was cracked and warped, and dark with age; it looked black in places. There was no fire just now in the great fireplace, but it looked as if it were used regularly.

It was a moment or so before the people had separated themselves in her mind into individuals, and by that time Marc was already introducing them, so that she had to listen fast to catch up:

". . . my sister, Berthe. She's the mother of the children you'll be minding. And Berthe's husband, Ralph. Hello, Ralph."

Ralph had a drink in one hand. Judging from his unsteady manner, it was far from his first of the day.

The children themselves hovered a short distance down the hall. Marc seemed not to notice them at all; certainly he made no attempt to introduce them. Only Antoinette seemed to notice them, and when she fixed her cold gaze upon them, they disappeared almost at once into one of the rooms off the hall, leaving Margaree with the adults of the family to contend with.

She greeted them a bit hesitantly. She was waiting, really, for their reaction to her. Not that she expected them to recognize her for the long lost relative she was, and fling open their arms. Even if they knew the truth, she could hardly expect open arms. But she had a tendency to wait and see how people took to her before she decided just how to act toward them.

They did not take very well to her. Her empty stare seemed to them implacable and even challenging, instead of expectant and awed, as it really was. It was not the first time shyness had been mistaken for hostility.

Berthe took her in with one long glance and decided that she did not like her. She dismissed her from her mind.

Ralph, lifting his glass aloft and spilling his drink

over the rim in the process, began a flowery speech of welcome that he had apparently been rehearsing:

"Welcome young lady to our fair castle."

That was as far as he got before Berthe interrupted him. She did it in such an offhand way that you saw at once she was accustomed to doing it often. Even he did not seem to be particularly surprised, although he fixed his bleary eyes on her.

"Jean is back," Berthe said. She spoke directly to her mother. None of the others seemed to matter very much to her.

"Yes," Antoinette said, busy at removing her white gloves with slow, elegant movements. "He left yesterday to come back on the train. He doesn't care for Marc's driving, it would seem."

"You aren't going to like what he's done," Berthe said. She looked nervous. But she did not look altogether unhappy with the present state of affairs. She seemed to catch the scent of impending trouble, and Margaree had the impression that it pleased her.

"He's had the piano taken out of the solarium. Some men were up just an hour or two ago to take it away. They took it right out of the house. I told them you wouldn't like it one bit, and they'd just have to bring it back, but Jean told them to take it along. It's gone, I've no idea where."

This announcement, delivered breathlessly, was greeted with a heavy silence, into which Jean Copley himself stepped a moment later.

Having met him once before, in the hotel in Boston, Margaree ought to have been prepared for him the second time. But she was not. She had seen him before where he was completely out of place. In the overstated elegance of that hotel suite he had looked rough and crude, even a bit coarse. But although this hall was elegant too, it suited him, with its worn tiles and blackened woods. He wore a tweed coat and was smoking an old pipe. He looked older and more in possession of himself.

He paused coming into the hall, and looked at her, and seemed as disconcerted by this second meeting as she was. He had his face tilted up, as if he were standing in dirty water neck high. The result was that he looked down his nose at her with a surprised look, as if he were trying to comprehend this apparition that had suddenly appeared in the shadows before him. And the dim lighting, the high ceiling far away in shadows, the echoing stillness, made the moment seem solemn to her. It was as if, for a moment, the others had faded away, and only the two of them were there, looking at each other. She had a silly impulse to run to him and tell him the truth, and ask him for the justice she had come seeking.

He was remarkably good-looking, far more so than she had remembered—tall and dark, thick browed. He looked somber, too, and quite formidable. He was not the sort of person you could just run to, at whose lapels one could catch. He would listen when it seemed right to him.

She did not try to say anything to him. It would have seemed superfluous just then.

The moment passed. The others came back into focus, and Antoinette spoke, making his dark eyes change colors slightly.

"Why did you have the piano taken out of the solarium?" she asked. Her tone was quite conversational, if a little cool.

"I needed money for the boat," he said. "I told you that."

"And I told you why I wouldn't give you the money," she said. "You must have the piano brought back."

"No one's touched that thing in fifteen years," he said. He was the only one in that group who seemed unintimidated by her. He alone seemed to feel himself her equal. And in a way, she too acted as if it were so. She moved more cautiously with him than with the others; she was not quite so sure of the success of her efforts.

"That has nothing to do with it," she said. "The room won't look right without it there."

"I sold the piano," he said. A crafty smile moved his lips. "But the man I sold it to will be happy to sell it back. For a right price."

She remembered then that Margaree was with them. Her cool eyes looked at the girl as if she wished she would disappear. When she did not, Antoinette turned sharply and moved down the hall.

"Come with me to the office," she said. "Marc,

you come too. Berthe, have Louise show this young lady to her room."

And so not only did Antoinette leave, disappearing into a room down the hall, but the others went too in her wake, all at once as it were, and Margaree was suddenly alone in that large hall. She had a strange feeling that she had been put in her place, for some reason that she could not fathom, reminded that she was a servant.

Her exhilaration, that had blazed so brightly upon her first arrival, had burned itself out. She felt the pain of being excluded, not at a distance as she had been all her life, but first hand. It was one thing as a young girl to entertain and solace oneself with the idea of being a disinherited princess; it was quite another thing to be here, and to be snubbed.

She thought of the scenes she had used to imagine, of when she would one day return home in glory. She thought of the welcomes she had fancied she would receive from the people who were, after all, her family. There would be embraces, questions, tender reproofs for staying away so long.

She took sides against herself, deliberately flogging herself by going farther and farther back, digging more and more painful imaginings. The beautiful Antoinette, unhappy, bent by the weight of her sins, weeping and begging forgiveness for the unhappiness she had caused; old servants recognizing her at once: "But you are the little child we all adored. You have come home!" The dispossessed princess returning to her throne in triumph.

She stood crushed with shame, neglected. She had come instead like a thief in the night, lying, disguising herself, skulking about, only to be treated as the servant she had made herself out to be.

She could not bear to stand in the face of her unhappiness, and she moved along the hall aimlessly. Her footsteps sounded loud to her own ears.

She was really alone for no more than a moment or so before a thin little girl in a maid's uniform came hurrying. She was Louise, apparently, sent to get her put into her right place quickly. The entire household reflected the moods and whims of its mistress unthinkingly. Louise was polite, but barely so. Margaree doubted that Antoinette Harrod would have stooped to instructing the girl to act in such a manner. Rather, the maid had merely absorbed it from the tone of voice in which her instructions had been given to her; it had not occurred to her to make any judgment of her own. This newcomer was a tutor, a governess. She was something a little more than a maid, true, but hardly on a level with the members of the family.

"This way, miss," she said; she opened one of a pair of doors in the south wall.

Beyond the doors was a stone passage—stone walled, stone floored. At the end of it stood a spacious circular staircase. It was rather a lovely affair, really. Half its circumference was a graceful stone open work, the other half solid outside wall into which had been cut two or three narrow windows that revealed its considerable thickness. The stone treads were worn treacherously. Margaree followed the maid's example and stayed close to the wall as they went up.

They went from the stone steps to a polished wooden floor that made creaking noises as they walked. The nearest door was open; the maid indicated it. Margaree went in, and she was suddenly quite alone. The maid disappeared as if on a vapor.

The room she was in was a small, cold one with the same darkly paneled walls she had seen below and a parquet floor over which had been thrown faded rugs. There was a small fireplace in one corner, where a fire had been laid but not lit. There was, besides the narrow uncomfortable looking bed, a chest of drawers, an armoire, a washstand with a basin and pitcher atop it, a badly battered wing chair, and just about enough room to turn around in. Her luggage, one largish trunk and a smaller bag that did not match, had been brought up, and stood beneath the single window. The curtains at the window were cotton to match the coverlet on the bed. It was little more than a cubbyhole, a far cry from what she used to imagine she would have when she returned to Stornoway.

"I've had a lot worse," she told herself.

It was true, but did very little to lift her spirits. It did not matter how much more something was, if it fell short of being enough.

She wondered how she would feel later, when

the lights were out, and this big old house started making its nighttime noises.

It was already growing dark. She thought about a bath, and wondered what arrangements there were. No one had said. She found some matches on the dresser, and lit one. The pitcher was empty on the washstand. No one had thought to bring water. There was a small door in the stand; not to her surprise she found that it concealed a nice white porcelain chamber pot that made her giggle despite herself.

The match burned her fingers, and she had to blow it out. She decided she would go exploring, and set off down the dim, creaking, ancient corridor. There was a smell of history in the stale, cold air. It was silent, but it was a silence that held the ghosts of other sounds that had been made centuries before.

She came to a door that stood open upon a room. She did not mean to, but the sight of it made her pause. It was spacious and lovely, all pink silk and gilt. Four vast windows in the south wall opened upon a misty, twilight view of the countryside looking away from the sea. The fire here had been lit and was glowing and flickering on the hearth. The pointed yellow and orange flames looked quite busy; while the dusk darkened rapidly, they lighted the tea things that had been set out on the table, and warmed the air.

It looked very much like the rooms her mother

had used to describe to her. It looked, in fact, quite like the room she had used to imagine would be hers. She came into it without thinking of whose it might be.

It was the first time in her life she had ever stood before an open fire.

For some mysterious reason, she began to cry.

CHAPTER 4

Jean Copley was both pleased and disappointed. He was pleased that he had wrested the money he needed from his mother. He was disappointed that it had been necessary to stoop to such distasteful stunts to get it. He did not care a great deal for money; certainly not for the Harrod money, and he used it as little as possible. He did not even as a rule live here at Stornoway, although it was ostensibly his home too. As often as not he stayed at the inn in the village. Sometimes he slept on the little fishing boat he owned and on which, for the most part, he earned his own living.

"Playing at being a fisherman," his mother called it, and his stepbrother Marc snickered as he always did when he thought his mother's remarks expected it.

But he did not regard that rugged, sometimes

dangerous combat with the sea as play. It was true, it was his greatest pleasure, but that was because he loved challenge and thrilled to danger. Hard work exhilarated him and even rested him, as no amount of leisure could.

But play, no. Soon, if luck ran with him, he would have the boat paid for, and would be truly able to make his own living without help from anyone else. Then he could say to Hell with the entire Harrod clan, and live the free life that he had dreamed of since he had been a child.

He came upstairs to his room. It was still regarded as his room at least, although he hadn't spent two of the last twenty nights in it.

He came down the upstairs hall quickly and quietly, walking on rubber-soled shoes so that he made almost no sound. Ahead of him the door to Berthe's room was open. He heard a movement inside; he knew that his stepsister was downstairs because he had just left her.

He came back to the open doorway, pausing in it. The newcomer was there, the girl with the sad look. She troubled him, that one, in a way that he did not fully comprehend. She had had a strange effect upon him that very first time he had seen her, in the hotel in Boston, but he could not describe satisfactorily to himself what that effect had been. He had seen Marc look the girl over on that occasion, as if she were a side of beef he were buying for the kitchen, and he, Jean had resented it. There was no need for him to do so. The girl was nothing to him, and she wouldn't be the first. There were few girls working around the house that Marc hadn't had a tumble with. But most of the girls who came into the service already had a look of experience about them. They recognized the gleam in Marc's eyes at once, and either they welcomed it, or they threw him a challenge. This girl had been different. She hadn't even seemed to know what the light in his stepbrother's eyes meant, and it had made Jean quite unaccountably want to protect her from it. And that impulse, completely foreign to him, had made him angry with the girl, so that he had behaved quite rudely.

And now, here she was, quite alone in his sister's room, where she would certainly get the devil for being, if she were found—and she was crying. Not the way he was used to seeing women cry, to get what they wanted out of a man, but softly and quite touchingly. He had an immediate and nearly overpowering urge to go to her and take her into his arms for comfort, and it never crossed his mind that it would be the first time his strong arms had ever played that role.

He did not, though, partly because he didn't understand or like these peculiar new impulses of his, and partly because it was too much like the sort of thing his stepbrother would do, with different motives, of course, and he did not want to be accused, even in his own mind, of behaving like Marc.

"Is something wrong?" he asked instead; his voice was gruff, because it was always gruff. It did not occur to him that the girl crying softly nearby would think it sounded angry. He was used to talking to sails and waves and rocks, and they didn't mind a harsh tone.

She started, swallowing hard and turned slowly, almost managing to look as if she hadn't been crying.

"I was looking for the bathroom," she blurted out, and was immediately embarrassed. It was stupid and schoolgirlish to blush as she was doing, and yet her face was crimson.

It would have helped if he had laughed, or made a joke. It would have helped if he had taken it all matter-of-factly. But the fact that he too seemed embarrassed and ill at ease only made it painfully worse.

"Oh," he said, his shoulders seeming to grow even stiffer. "Along here."

He led the way. She followed in his footsteps like a little shadow, watching the dim shadows play across his broad shoulders and tapering back. Despite the fact that the house was big, and the hall oversized too, he looked too big for the place. She kept expecting his head to scrape the ceiling or his shoulders to bump the walls on either side. She had to hurry to keep up with him, although his pace looked leisurely to watch.

He went along the right hand turn of the passage to a door at the end, reaching inside to turn on a switch. "The lavatory's here," he said, avoiding her embarrassed look. "The bath is just around the corner on the left as you come back. I'll leave the door open for you, so you can find it."

He left, moving swiftly and silently, as if eager to be away from her. That at least was the impression he gave her. It was partly true. He was eager to be away, because she disturbed him. But as soon as he was out of sight of her, he found himself thinking of her, and wanting to see her again. In his own room, he succeeded in convincing himself that it was because there was something oddly familiar about her; perhaps they had met sometime before, although the likelihood seemed slim.

She walked back along the dim passage. He had left the door to the bath open. It was a room considerably larger than her bedroom.

While she was out someone had come to her room and brought hot water in a copper can, and a pair of lighted candlesticks. They gave the room a pale light. The fire still had not been lit, although it was now evening and rapidly growing cold.

She washed in the hot water and dressed for dinner. She had a dress of gray velvet in her trunk. It had been her mother's, and had been made over years ago for her to wear to a nearly forgotten party. The design was simple enough that it did not look terribly out of date, and the color did wonderful things for her. Ordinarily she kept her hair pulled neatly back, but because she was tired and the lighting was poor in her room, she left it fall loosely about her shoulders, brushed until it was a shimmering cloud of pale gold.

No one had told her when dinner was, or if she was expected to join them. In the books she had read, the governess commonly did join the family for meals.

She sat for a time huddled before the unlit fire. She had lived too long in the world, earning her own way, not to know how to endure slights and rebuffs, although she could still be hurt by them. Finally, she got up and went downstairs by the same stairs she had used before. It was lighted by a hanging lamp.

She followed the ground-floor passage to the great entrance hall. The hearth here was still dark, but another hanging lamp valiantly struggled to light the great expanse.

She hesitated here, because all the doors were closed, and she had no idea where to go. But just then Jean came through a pair of doors in the north wall.

She had no way of knowing that it was unusual for him to have stayed for dinner, let alone to have dressed as he did, or that it had been only for her sake.

"So you found it," he said. "I was coming to look for you." He meant it to be friendly. But his manner was naturally rough, and she was in a sensitive state, ready to be slighted, so that it sounded very inhospitable to her. She chose not to reply at all.

He watched her coming toward him, very slowly, looking like a moonbeam in her gray velvet. The beauty of her touched some spot of softness within him that had been untouched heretofore. He felt completely stupid and clumsy. His hands and feet seemed to be in the way. For the only time in his life he envied Marc his elegant graciousness.

Marc gave her a look that was more than approving. "How lovely," he murmured.

Ralph was having yet another drink. His eyes twinkled a bit too brightly. "A vision of loveliness," he said, slurring the words a little. "Welcome to our family circle."

Berthe looked once at her, frowned a little, and looked away without speaking.

She had come into a lovely room, long and dark and rich in ornaments. The ceiling and walls were squares of dark, intricately carved wood. Each of the shorter end walls held chimney pieces of sculptured stone, but the stone was of such a grace and delicacy that they became ornaments for a drawing room rather than merely functional pieces.

The room was warm, deliciously warm. On both of the hearths magnificent fires had been lighted; the warmth and light moved boldly out from each of them, to meet in the center of the room.

"Something to drink?" Marc asked her. When she hesitated, he added, "Some sherry?"

She gave him a grateful smile and nodded. She knew very little about those things, but she knew that her mother had used to drink sherry. When he brought it, she found that it had a pleasant nutlike flavor, and it seemed to give her a bit of her strength back.

They were all of them waiting, and in a short time, Antoinette came in. She swept into a room, and even a stranger would have known at once that she was mistress here. She had recovered completely from the fatigue of the long drive home; indeed, she looked as if she had grown younger and more beautiful. The house, the candlelight, the dancing fires, all suited her. Her dark hair danced with blue lights. Her eyes were like twin onyx, her skin like the palest of alabaster. She wore a dress of blood-red silk that no one else in the world could have worn with such success.

Margaree, who had thought until then that she looked nice, felt ugly and coarse in comparison. She could well understand how men had been persuaded to treachery and cruelty by this woman.

Antoinette's eyes went at once to Jean, and widened a little. "This is an honor," she said. "To what do we owe it?"

Her eyes fell on Margaree then, as if she had forgotten her altogether. Her expression changed, effectively discouraging any answer to the question she had asked. Jean looked angry; Marc looked amused.

As if everything had been waiting the right cue, the double door on the other side of the room opened almost at once, and the butler appeared to announce dinner.

The dining room was a different sort of room,

pleasant, but in a massive and simple, even severe, style. The floor and walls were stone, the latter whitewashed, and the ceiling had exposed beams. The fireplace was by the door, so that when Margaree came in she saw not it, but the warm waves of firelight that splashed gently against the white walls and fell softly back, like an ancient tide.

She had eaten hundreds, probaby thousands of meals, and for as long as she could remember they had been in drab, tiny kitchens that were too cold or too hot. But the dinners of her past had been eaten in atmospheres of some happiness and affection. She felt stifled by the atmosphere in this room. It was not only directed against her. The people at the table did not care for one another in any warm way.

Not that there was open hostility, except from and toward Jean, who seemed to give as much disfavor as he got. They were polite and superficially friendly, and there was an even flow of conversation.

Margaree did not take part in most of it; very little of it was directed at her, or even acknowledged her presence. There was some talk of a maid who had had to be let go, and Berthe asked a question or two about Boston, using a tone that made plain she was annoyed that she hadn't been asked to go along.

Marc made an effort to include Margaree in some talk. He explained, in answer to her question, that the children did not eat with the family.

"It would hamper our elegant conversation," he said. This was added in a tone that mocked the triviality of the conversation that had preceded it.

"The children take their meals at an earlier hour," Antoinette said, hardly glancing up from her plate. "It seems best for them, as this hour suits me best. You'll meet them soon enough."

"No need to hasten to chores," Marc said.

"I enjoy children," Margaree said.

The conversation faltered.

"We used to stay at another hotel in Boston," Marc said, changing the subject. "The Dublin. A nice place. But they had a big ruckus a while back about ghosts. The place was said to be haunted. And mother announced we couldn't stay there any more."

Margaree looked toward Antoinette. It was so incongruous to think of that self-possessed woman afraid of ghosts that she thought Marc must be making another joke. But Antoinette did not look at all amused, nor did she seem to approve of Margaree's smile. Margaree quickly grew solemn again.

"We changed hotels," Antoinette said, "Because I did not like all of the publicity the Dublin received, and which I personally suspected they courted. Have you lived in the city all of your life, Miss Butler? I believe you told us Carver?"

"Carver, yes," Margaree said. "It's a bit small as cities go."

"But still a bit different from our isolation. I hope this will not be too lonely for you."

"I spent some time in the country once," Margaree said after a moment's hesitation. "With the family of a girl I went to school with."

"A farm?" Ralph asked, stirring himself to make a contribution to the talk.

"Not exactly," Margaree said.

"Stornoway is not exactly a farm either," Ralph said, and seemed to be amused by his own remark. He chuckled and had another drink of wine.

"We have animals," Berthe said. "Pigs."

Margaree, eager to keep this silly conversation alive, because even a stupid conversation was better than sitting ignored as she had been, said all too quickly, "I adore pigs."

The conversation came to an abrupt halt.

Jean stepped into the silence. "We keep no livestock," he said flatly.

She saw then what the remark had meant, and felt completely foolish. Her face reddened, and she concentrated upon her food, and did not try to enter the conversation again.

Again, Jean seemed to try to rescue her, in his clumsy way. When the silence had become embarrassing, he suddenly asked a question of his mother and she, looking quite surprised for a change, answered at more length than was her custom. The conversation resumed, and Margaree felt less the foolish center of attention.

She knew that Jean had deliberately tried to ease her embarrassment, and she was curious. During the rest of the meal she studied him covertly, trying to fathom him. He had dressed, but even so he looked coarse and unpolished among the others. He might as well have been wearing his old tweed jacket. Not that she minded his appearance; far from it. He had an exhilarating masculinity that frightened her not with a fear of him, but of herself. He was very physical. She had never been in love nor involved in any sort of romance, except in her imagination. She had had dreams of handsome princes, usually associated with her return to Stornoway. They were dazzled by her, and bowed to her, and at the very most, held her hand. She had never imagined a man kissing her, had never thought about the feel of a man's powerful arms about her. But suddenly she thought of them now.

The bold lines of his face seemed more handsome to her each time she saw him. They were too strong; they jarred at first. But when the eye grew accustomed, they made others seem pale in contrast. She liked the dark brows that almost came together, and the severe carving of his nose, and the deep set of his eyes. When he talked, he had a habit of looking away, as if embarrassed. The harshness of his features was softened by a shadowy inward look that gave him a dreaming quality, the look of a poet almost. Once he laughed at something that had been said, and it was such an honest laugh that she smiled with it.

She looked up to see his dark eyes on her, and was embarrassed again. She looked away, into the fire, that great glowing cave that had framed flames for hundreds of years. It seemed natural to her, but nothing else quite did.

They went back to the drawing room for coffee, but the conversation had grown sparser. They had exhausted it during dinner without laying the groundwork for further talk. Ralph had sunk into a stupor and scarcely tried at all to rouse himself. Marc looked as if he had gotten bored. Margaree felt that he would like to go, but did not yet think the time right. Berthe seemed petulant; she wore that expression constantly. For all her servile manner toward her mother, Margaree thought that Berthe resented her mother's dominance far more than Marc did. Marc had learned after a manner to cope with it, so that within the confines of it he still enjoyed a considerable freedom. But Berthe's spirit was incapable of soaring. She seemed to resent Marc's freedom too, as if he had somehow acquired it at the expense of hers.

It was not a warm gathering. Margaree had the impression they were only waiting to be dismissed, like so many servants. Antoinette sipped coffee and seemed in no hurry to retire yet.

Jean did not wait to be dismissed with the others. He had become restless and even more ill at ease. At last he got up and went toward the door.

"Will you be staying the night?" Antoinette asked.

"At the glass house," he said. "Good night," he said to Margaree, and went out.

When he had gone, Antoinette said to Margaree,

"I suppose you're wondering what he meant by the glass house?"

"Yes, I was," she said, lying. She had really no need to wonder, since she already knew of the glass house, but she realized a bit late that that knowledge was a mistake, and pretended a great curiosity, even leaning forward a little in her chair.

"Old Mr. Harrod—that would be my husband's father—had a cottage built on the cliffs many years ago."

This, for no reason Margaree could discern, captured Ralph's attention, and he quoted Shakespeare, to Antoinette's annoyance: "The self same sun that shines upon his court Hides not his visage from our cottage, but looks on alike."

Antoinette went on as if he had not spoken. "People called it the glass house because almost one entire side of it—the sea side—is windows. It's quite impractical, with the storms we get here, but it does give a spectacular view. There was another son then, who was married. The cottage was intended for them. But that son died before they even got moved into the cottage."

It was difficult for Margaree not to show the pain these remarks caused her. It was almost as if those eyes watching her so keenly knew that the other son she spoke of was Margaree's father; that it was for him and Margaree's mother that the glass house had been built. She knew that she had to say something in reply, and she said finally, "How sad."

She hoped the conversation would not long continue in this vein.

Antoinette finished her coffee, finally, and there was a sudden flurry of movement as she signaled that she was done. The atmosphere seemed to relax all at once. Everyone looked a little less wary. They said good nights, lingering at the door.

"Will I meet the children tomorrow?" Margaree asked.

"In the morning." It was Antoinette who answered the question, not Berthe. Berthe seemed to have little voice in the question of raising her children; but then she seemed to have little interest in the subject as well. Antoinette managed that as she apparently managed everything else.

"I hope I'll meet Mr. Harrod too," Margaree added. She meant it quite sincerely. Yves Harrod was her closest living relative. Jean was not related to her at all, except by the chance of his mother's marriage, and that was more or less Ralph's position too. Marc and Berthe were Antoinette's offspring as well as vassals. But Yves, however weak and foolish he might have been as a young man, was her father's brother. Sooner or later the truth of who she was must come out, and she would need him for an ally then.

Her comment was met with coolness. "Perhaps," was all Antoinette said.

Margaree might have imagined it, but she thought the others exchanged glances. They seemed to be holding back. She went out into the cold hall, and the door swung softly shut after her with the others still in the drawing room. Almost at once, beyond the closed door, she heard their voices in a muted but animated conversation, far more lively than any that had taken place in her presence.

She crossed the hall and walked down the passage to the circular staircase. The hanging lamp there swayed in the path of a wayward breeze, casting ominous shadows through the brass openwork of its shade.

She paused at the bottom of the steps. For a moment it had seemed as if one of the shadows had separated itself from the others and moved with a life of its own. She caught her breath sharply, and stared upward with wide eyes.

But there was nothing after all. Her imagination was playing tricks on her, stirred by the conversation earlier of ghosts.

Antoinette believes in ghosts, she thought in a burst of revelation; that was why she had disapproved of Marc's reference to them earlier.

Probably, she thought, going up through the shadows, she had much to haunt her.

She came to her own room and went in. She was disappointed in herself and in the evening. The entire enterprise seemed foolish as well as dishonest, and she was assailed with doubts and fears of every sort. It was not right to be doing what she was doing. Even granting that it might be right, she wasn't up to the task. The sound of her own shrill, nervous voice echoed in her ears painfully. Her room looked cold and dark and no bigger than a closet. She felt rejected by the world, and no better for realizing that she had invited all this upon herself. She did not have to be here. She had had a job, a part time one, in Carver, and a dingy apartment on which she would have been able to afford the rent for the better part of a year. She could be hard at work right now making friends, meeting people, learning to live with the world on its own terms. She had lived too long with her mother's bitterness and her mother's sad memories of the past. It gave her a pang of guilt to think this, but it was true nonetheless. Her mother had needed a friend so badly that they had been sole friends to each other. Her mother had been so very unhappy that she had tried to lighten that burden by taking a great portion of it upon herself. It had stayed. She was utterly friendless now, and quite unhappy. She hadn't even the motivation to light a light, to move, or go to bed. She felt lifeless as well as motionless.

Someone shouted outside. She went to the window in the dark, bumping against the chest of drawers as she did so. The curtain smelled stale. Outside there was moonlight, and the house looked younger and lovelier than in daylight. In the pale stone courtyard Jean Copley was a dark, foreshortened shadow.

He had shouted to a dog, and the dog, a great shaggy brute of a thing, came joyously to meet him, bounding about with such fervor that he came not in a straight line, but zigzagging giddily across the open space. The man stooped to greet him, and they seemed to have an eager conversation about something. When he straightened and began to walk quickly away, the dog trotted happily alongside him. They disappeared under the stone roof of the porch.

She felt about and found matches on the table with which to light the candles. With another she lit the fire, and sat down before it. The rustle of burning paper was replaced with the roar of kindling. The flame flared, dropped a little, and began to burn in earnest. The warmth crept out into the room, and in its glow, she began to feel angry.

She had not asked to be born, but she had been. She was alive and human, and she had rights. She had a right to be here. This was at least as much her home as theirs, anyone would agree to that. She would establish that fact once and for all, she would make them welcome her as a member of the family, and not as some shoddy outsider without even a decent dinner dress.

But beneath all this was a sadness as soft and bitter as smoke curling around her heart. When she went to bed at last she cried, for the first time ever, over the injustice of her life, and wished that she had died instead of her mother.

While she slept, both she and the house stirred uneasily, as if waiting for something to happen. In her room, Antoinette Harrod stared through the dim light, for she never slept without a light in her room, at the silk canopy over her bed, and wondered how best to deal with the threat of Margaree's presence.

The telephone by the bed made a faint jingling sound. She knew its meaning. She had discovered quite by accident that it made that sound when someone was calling out on one of the other phones.

She reached for the instrument and took it up with no pang of conscience. Everything that went on in Stornoway was her affair. She listened in silence while Marc made a date with some village tart, frowning at the telephone receiver in distaste. But she did not interfere. When her son had hung up, she did the same, and promptly dismissed the matter from her mind. She thought Marc a fool. She did not disparage the satisfaction of those physical urges; she was no automaton. But the clever person made use of such desires. Sex was such a useful tool in accomplishing one's goals, that it was foolish to expend it profitlessly.

Having made his arrangements, Marc slept. He had lingering thoughts of the naïve-looking governess who had come so unexpectedly into the picture of their life here. He took it for granted that he would be able to seduce her, in due time.

Berthe tried to close her ears and her mind to her husband's violent snoring. She tried to take her mind off him, but none of the people or things she thought about were any more pleasing to her. She resented Marc, who aways seemed to get his way, when she never got hers. She loathed Jean, most of all, because he lived quite free of Stornoway, and Antoinette, and always did just as he pleased. She hated and feared Antoinette, and at the same time wished she were more like her. She disliked the new governess, for her slim grace.

She wished she were away from here, anywhere else but Stornoway.

Ralph snored.

In the glass house Jean grew impatient with himself because he could not sleep. He was stirred by thoughts of pale yellow hair and the soft look of that girl's skin.

Margaree woke once with a start. She could not think at first what it was that had roused her, but at last she thought she knew. The door of her room had closed with a click of the latch.

Her skin tingled. The thought that someone had been watching her and had gone was somehow more frightening than to waken and find someone there.

She got up and, shivering partly because the fire had gone out, went to the door and opened it.

The hall was empty, but again there was that impression of just missing something, of someone or something just out of the range of vision. She thought she heard scurrying footsteps in the distance, but it might have been only her imagination again.

There was no lock on her door. She closed it firmly, and went back to bed.

CHAPTER 5

She woke to a day that was as gray as the stones of the house. No matter, she knew what she had to do. She had faced the idea the night before, and when she woke the decision was already clear in her mind. She was not going to slink around like some sort of thief, pretending to be a servant, a nobody, and begging for crumbs of their attention. She meant to tell them who she was, and take her chances on what happened after that. If she were thrown bodily out of the place, which was very much within the realm of possibility—well, she had tried to do what her mother wanted, at least, and she could leave with a clear conscience, and be done with it.

Or almost be done with it. She went to the window and looked out at the courtyard. She could not delude herself. She loved Stornoway. It was in her blood, and that first glimpse of it yesterday had been enough to seal her fate. She would always love it, always want it. Perhaps it was a result of her mother's old tales, perhaps it was because Stornoway symbolized all her childhood dreams.

Jean came into the courtyard below, crossing it quickly, and went out of sight.

Very well, she thought, turning from the window and beginning to dress. Perhaps she could not just go away; perhaps she was deluding herself about that. But she would not stay as an impostor either. What could they do after all? They couldn't just lock her in the dungeon, assuming that there was one.

At least, she didn't think they could.

She wore a dress that had once been a rich navy blue, and was now faded to the color of denim. With her hair pulled back, she looked like a little girl instead of a young woman. She did not know it, but it made her look all the more in need of a man's protection.

She went downstairs and through the great hall, to the outside, following the sound of voices. Although the hall had been bitterly cold, the day outside was mild.

Antoinette was there, explaining something in definite terms to Marc.

Margaree said, "Good morning," as she came out. She took a stand on the steps, thrusting her hands deep into the pockets of her skirt, planting her feet wide apart, as if they might try to drag her away.

They turned, saying "Good morning" in unison, as if they had practiced it. Antoinette left her son without excusing herself and came toward Margaree.

"Come with me, please," she said. She went on without hesitation, merely taking it for granted that Margaree would follow.

She did so, inside again, through the hall, back into the passage. They went past the staircase, into a number of bare rooms, and through them. Antoinette walked with the grace of a swan and the precision of a soldier. Margaree moved along after her, feeling clumsy as she watched the beautiful dark head and the proud shoulders.

They came into a room that was furnished rather as an office, with two desks, and chairs, and a great many books on shelves.

"This will do for a classroom," Antoinette said. "I shall have Berthe bring the children down shortly."

"I want to talk to you," Margaree said. It was difficult to speak up to this overpowering creature. "To all of you, I mean. The whole family, together." She had no intention of making her painful confession more than once.

"In that case," Antoinette said, taking the announcement as calmly as she seemed to take everything else, "It had best wait until lunch. It's difficult enough to get them all together then. I have no intention of attempting it at this peculiar hour of the day."

And in that manner, she pointed out that Margaree had slept later than was usual in the house.

"I'll have the children brought," she said, and turned to leave her.

"I haven't had any breakfast," Margaree said in her tiniest voice. She felt miserable again.

"You haven't had breakfast?" Antoinette looked directly at her, and repeated this in a manner that suggested Margaree might be lying on this point. Her eyes were cold and sharp. "Didn't you ring when you wakened?"

"There isn't a bell in my room," Margaree said. She hadn't looked, but she felt confident it was true. The walls of her room were painfully unadorned.

"Where did they put you?"

"In—in a little room, overlooking the courtyard."

Quite unexpectedly, Antoinette laughed, so that Margaree suddenly realized that she must have known all along which room; the servants wouldn't have dared to put her there unless they had been specifically instructed to.

"Don't you like little rooms then?" she asked, and it was such a cruel form of amusement that Margaree did not reply at all and barely managed to keep her face expressionless.

"Oh, well, I suppose you must be fed," Antoinette said, her smile fading again. "I'll have something brought in here for you."

She started away.

"I'll have coffee and toast, please," Margaree said, exactly as one would give a waitress an order in a coffee shop, carelessly, authoritatively.

Antoinette stopped, her hand on the handle of the door, and Margaree fully expected those dark eyes to rake over her in anger. But the older woman only pulled her shoulders back a little more firmly, and went on.

Margaree turned from the door, but she felt sick rather than triumphant. She hadn't wanted to be as unkind as they were, and she certainly didn't need to make any more of an enemy of Antoinette than she already was. She had only wanted to show that she wasn't a servant, that she needn't crawl. She had done it badly, though. Antoinette would not soon forget or forgive being treated as if she were a servant.

She looked at the room. It was lovely, as all of the rooms were here—at least, all of the rooms that were furnished. There was a fire framed in brick and copper, and above it a glum-looking man of oil and canvas. The sun was fighting through the clouds outside, and traced the outlines of the windows across the floor.

A plump girl in a maid's uniform brought a tray. It held coffee and toast—exactly that, and nothing more. No butter, no jam, no cream or sugar.

There was a note, too. It said, in a powerful hand; *You may have lunch with the family.*

She was being given, as a crumb, what was hers by right, and again reminded that she was a servant. She remembered her mother, how bitter she had been at times, how resentful and suspicious, looking out at a world that she had regarded as hostile. For the first time Margaree seemed to stand in her mother's place, to look out at the world through the same defensive eyes. She knew, as her mother must have known, her own powerlessness.

She collected her anger, and made a weapon of it. She would not remain blocked and frustrated. She would not be intimidated. Integrity was on her side, and she believed in its ultimate power.

She ate hurriedly, gulping down the dry toast and washing it out of her mouth with the coffee. She wanted that necessity out of the way, and its scant nourishment within her, before the battle.

Time passed. She paced back and forth, from the hearth to the glass doors at the opposite end of the room, and back again. Beyond the doors the terrace was bright now with sunlight. Another time she would have liked to go out in it. She looked at her watch and paced some more.

And time passed. She went back and forth along the windows. At the opposite end of the terrace, tall columns supported the roof. They cast delicate shadows on the weathered stone.

The curtains were silk, deep blue. They framed

the view. In the distance she could see the ocean, and far away the misty horizon. The sky was clouding over again. The morning was nearly over.

Beyond the glass house, wooden steps led downward to Harrod Cove, and the private little beach that belonged to Stornoway.

Berthe was there now, sitting in a folding canvas chair that looked altogether inadequate for her mass. She looked skyward and glowered at the sun's disappearance behind the clouds. She glowered too at her children, playing quietly on the rocky beach. She wished perversely that they would make some loud noise, or do something out of the way, so that she could shout at them. But they defied her by remaining quiet and innocent.

There was only Ralph to vent her anger upon. He was sleeping beside her. Although he was as quiet as a mouse, she kicked his foot with hers and said, "Wake up, you're snoring."

He sat up a bit groggily. "Ah, sleep," he said, yawning. "So like death, I dare not trust it."

"It's like death with you," she said. "The only way I'll know when you've died is that you won't be snoring. And don't you start quoting poetry at me either. Where are you going?"

"I thought I'd take the boat out," he said, walking toward a shack standing near the cliffs. She looked resentfully after him, but she let him go.

He lowered the boat, only a small rowboat, into the water, and began to row out of the cove.

"Don't you go far," she yelled after him, sorry now that she hadn't forbidden him to go altogether. "It's almost lunchtime."

"Just around the bend," he called back, rowing energetically. "Some birds are nesting there, and I wish to see their homely progress."

When he was around the bend, and out of sight, he pulled the oars into the boat and let it drift. Getting down on his knees, he felt under the wooden seat, and found the package he had hidden there, a bottle of whiskey cushioned in several sacks.

He lay back in the boat and drank from the bottle. The whiskey warmed its way down through his body, seeming to release some of the tension he had felt building up within himself.

"If die I must," he quoted softly to himself, "let me die drinking . . ."

No one came into the room where Margaree waited. Not the children, not Berthe, not even the maid to clear the tray away. And at last she realized that no one would come. This was the further insult, leaving her here alone in this room, with nothing to do but wait until lunch when she had been given permission to dine with the family.

It was already lunchtime when she finally realized this. At first she rejected the idea because it seemed too rude even for this unfriendly household. But at last she saw that it was so, and her anger boiled up in her like a pot left too long on the stove. It ran over, and brought her storming out of that room, through the other, bare rooms, along the halls. She came into the drawing room virtually on Antoinette's elegant heels, and might have shoved that lovely woman out of the way had it been necessary to do so.

Scarcely pausing for breath she said in a high, unsteady voice, "My name is Margaree Butler Harrod. I am a Harrod, Waldo Harrod's daughter. This is my home, my inheritance, that you cheated me out of. I have a right to be here, and I am going to stay here, in that awful little cubbyhole of a room if I must. You will have to drag me out of this place if you mean to get rid of me."

The silence following this announcement was punctuated by the sound of her uneven breathing. She had practically run all the way here from that room in which she had been left to cool her heels through the morning.

Only Antoinette seemed unsurprised by this outburst. Margaree turned on her; for once she was not intimidated by that cool gaze.

"And that," Margaree said, "is what I wanted to tell everyone this morning."

In the end, however, it was Antoinette's icy calm that undid her. She was prepared for battle. She was not prepared for being treated exactly the same as before, as if she were a servant, or worse still, a tempermental child.

"Go to your room," Antoinette said in a low voice that was nonetheless commanding. "We'll discuss this later."

She went, because that unfaltering confidence was greater than her own shaky faith. "I won't leave," she said, but less sharply. "I'm staying at Stornoway."

She went back out, up to her own room, slamming the door of it hard. For once she was glad of the smallness of her room. It gave a protective feeling.

Some of the momentum had gone out of her. Now that it was done, she could look back upon the burning bridges and wonder if she had been wise to set fire to them. She had no doubt that the Harrods were angry; looked at from their point of view, they had a right to be. They had been tricked, after all; hardly a decent beginning for the re-establishing of old family ties.

She hadn't been there long when Marc opened the door without knocking and came in. He looked like he had come to scold her, and she immediately went on the defensive again, thrusting out her chin like a stubborn child.

"Well," he said, lighting a cigarette, "you've rocked the boat, haven't you, dear cousin?"

"What did she say?" Margaree asked. She felt certain they had discussed her outburst, however briefly. And for all her stubborn demeanor, she was afraid of what that strong woman downstairs would do now.

"She wasn't happy," he said. He smiled. "That's putting it mildly, as a matter of fact."

"And I suppose she's sent you up to do her dirty work," she said angrily.

This new outspokenness seemed to make him thoughtful. He surveyed her. He did not attempt to conceal a certain interest in her physical loveliness, but she was too angry to pay much attention to the movement of his eyes up and down her body.

"It must hurt you to be treated like an outcast," he said a trifle hesitantly.

"It isn't right," she said.

He shrugged.

"And you don't care, I suppose, whether something is right or not? You don't care what sort of dirty work you're asked to do, you just hold your nose and plunge in? And the head of the household stands high and untouchable, shielded from everything unpleasant . . ."

He laughed lightly; he seemed to find the entire situation more amusing than unpleasant.

"Why bark at me," he said. "As you say, heads of households. They will have their way. She's a law unto herself here, and anyway, you have no case. You have no real proof of any claim, have you? There's a moral obligation, I suppose, but if she chooses to ignore that . . ."

Something crossed Margaree's mind. "I want to see my uncle," she said impulsively.

"Yves?" He looked quite surprised by this suggestion, and not at all pleased. "I don't think that would be very wise."

She noted that he had said "Yves," and not "my father."

"He is the real head of the household, isn't he?"

"You've been told, though. He isn't well. And as far as that goes, no, he isn't head of the household. Antoinette rules here. He would never do anything against her."

She had a sinking sensation. Until then, he had remained as an ally to whom she might be able to turn. Shadowy, of course, tentative, but at least a potential ally.

"She's made him a slave, you mean," she said.

He shrugged. "He isn't well. Leave it at that, and don't ask to see him. Anyway,"—his expression changed and became less argumentative—"anyway, it isn't necessary. I might be able to help you. My mother isn't so immovable that she can't be persuaded—by her favorite son."

This turnabout caught her off guard. She had been exposed to the world enough that she ought to have been suspicious. But she wanted help too badly, to question it when it came.

"You'd help me?" she asked eagerly.

"I might," he said. He put his cigarette out in an ashtray, smearing it slowly about until the glow was completely gone. He took a step toward her. "If you coaxed me a little," he added.

He took hold of her then, a bit roughly, as if she already belonged to him, and pulled her toward him.

Under other circumstances, she might have

reacted more willingly. He was handsome, after all, and a kiss was only a kiss, not a contract to go any further.

But something in the way he seized her was all wrong. It was as if she were still the servant, and he the master of the house. The kiss he was preparing to bestow upon her was not the kiss of love or affection, nor even of respectful desire, but the presumptuous kiss of the *seigneur*, and she resented it at once, and tried to pull away from him.

He was stronger than he looked, and her reluctance, far from discouraging him, seemed to whet his appetite. "Hold still," he said sharply, his breath quickening.

"Let her go," someone said from behind her.

For a moment they remained as they were. Then, with another quick shrug and a grin, Marc did as he had been ordered. She looked over her shoulder, and saw Jean in the open doorway.

"We were only discussing what I could do to help our young cousin out of the predicament she's in," Marc said.

"Get out," Jean said. He said it quietly, but in a tone of voice that defied any argument. Marc hesitated for a moment only. Then, stepping sideways around his half brother, he got out of the room, and left without another word.

She was still angry, more so even than before, and she tried to take her anger out on Jean, simply because he was there.

"I'm not going," she said, nearly shouting.

"You'll have to have me arrested to get me out of here. And then I'll camp on your doorstep. I'll be round your necks as long as you live. I . . ."

"I understand," he said quite calmly. "But I don't think any of that will be necessary. She didn't say you would have to go."

"But he said . . ."

"He wanted you to think that. He wanted you to need his favor."

"But why . . . oh." She let it lie there. Her face reddened a little when she realized how cruelly he had tried to play upon her naïveté and her insecurity. But her defiance had collapsed in the face of Jean's air of sympathy, as defiance will do. Everything blurred. She felt gratitude toward this handsome man before her. The moment dimmed and lost reality. He seemed to loom over her, larger than life.

He had never found himself in a situation like this before, nor expected he ever would. He had fought with his family before, but always for his own personal ends. He had never imagined himself someone else's champion. He did not quite know what he wanted or should do next. He felt like taking her in his arms, but that was too like what Marc had just tried to do.

"Well," he said, as if answering some question she had asked, "there isn't much I can do. I'm not very much in favor here myself. Personally I can't think why you would want to stay, in this house, with these people. But I can see that you have a right, and I'll do what I can as long as you want to stay." He paused for a long moment, as if he found what else he had to say distasteful, but thought it ought to be said anyway.

"I don't mean in return for any favors," he said, looking away from her when he said it.

"I know," she said. She felt suddenly breathless. With a little sense of shock she realized with her conscious mind that another part of her had been wishing it had been him who had taken her in his arms. But obviously he had no such inclination. He was already stepping backward into the hall.

"Actually," he said, looking past her around the room, as if he were seeing it for the first time, "It's one of the best rooms in the place. It's small, and so it can be heated. Everyone else freezes to death."

He went, closing the door. She felt suddenly warm and safe in her little room, the best in the place, which was going to be really hers for a while. Perhaps forever.

She had not had lunch, and she was suddenly aware of being hungry. But she could not go down now and face the rest of them, if anything was left of the luncheon scene. For the present, she could live on her happiness. True, it was still clouded. She was hardly accepted into the family, let alone recognized as the rightful mistress of Stornoway. But she had accomplished so much with the simple act of honesty that she felt herself an entirely different person from the one she had been the day before.

She was so pleased with the way things had gone,

that she could not even be appropriately annoyed when she discovered that someone had been through her things in the dresser. They were somewhat disarranged, enough to tell her that someone had been looking through them.

"One of the maids, I suppose," she told herself, and shrugged it off. There was nothing much for anyone to steal, since she owned virtually nothing of any value, and she attributed it to nothing more than curiosity about a newcomer in the house.

Much later, she discovered that something was missing after all. But it was such a curious thing that she could not quite bring herself to accept the idea that it had been stolen, and ended by concluding that she must have somehow mislaid it when she had been packing to come here.

After all, why should anyone want to steal a black and white photograph of herself in a dime-store brass frame, that her mother had used to keep atop her chest of drawers.

The photograph had been taped to a wall in a large room in a tower in the opposite wing of the big house. The man in that room was seated on a stool, staring up at the photograph. It had been put up so that he had to look up to see it.

Despite this source of discomfort, he had been staring at the picture unceasingly for hours.

"You must remember this girl's face," Antoinette had told him when she put the photograph on the wall. "She is an enemy."

The girl was an enemy, that pale young thing smiling so innocently but deceptively down upon him. He did not understand why or how she was, but it was not necessary that he understand things. Antoinette understood, and she had said the girl was an enemy. Whatever she said, he accepted without question.

It was a pretty face. She looked very young, this enemy. And there was something about her that lingered at the back of his memory, like a word on the tip of the tongue, that one cannot quite call forth. There was a haunting familiarity about that smile, and the look in her eyes.

"Someday soon, my pet," Antoinette told him, running her fingers through his hair, "you may have to do something for me, something to make me happy.

Her voice was a crooning that made him feel content.

"Would you like that?" she asked. "To make Antoinette happy?"

He beamed and bobbed his head. The girl in the picture was an enemy, and he must memorize her face so that he would know her when he saw her, and out of all this, somehow, he would make Antoinette happy.

He only lived to make Antoinette happy.

CHAPTER 6

Margaree saw that things had changed for her when the maid, the plain dark one they called Louise, brought her some lunch on a tray. Antoinette must have ordered that done, and it seemed to signify that she was no longer one of the servants, but a member of the household. Too, Louise seemed to reflect a change in the attitude of her mistress. She was less distant and more friendly. She built up the fire before she went.

When she came back for the tray, she said, "Madame wishes to see you."

Margaree did not want to go. Anger had given her the courage to brave Antoinette, but her anger had faded. Now she was only relieved that she was going to be allowed to stay, and relief is not a powerful emotion that motivates action.

Of course she had to do as bidden, afraid or not.

"This way," Louise said. She led her through several rooms that were bare of furnishings to a door that revealed another little spiral staircase. There was darkness above and below the tiny triangular landing.

At Louise's instructions, she went down into the darkness, groping her way cautiously because it was steep and worn, and dangerous.

She emerged into the room in which she had been that morning. Antoinette was there, sitting at the writing table. She did not look particularly angry. In fact, she apologized almost before Margaree came into sight, although she did so coolly.

"I'm sorry that your homecoming should have been so insensitive," she said, glancing up. "Of course, not knowing who you were . . ." She left it hanging in the air, so that it was Margaree who was made guilty for the inadequacies of her own welcome.

But she did not mind, any more than she minded the coolness of this apology. She was here, and she had gotten the apology, and that was vastly more than she had had any right to imagine she would achieve.

"It was foolish of me to have come back in that way," she said. "Forgive me."

"I'm surprised that, if you expected us to be that inhospitable, you should have wanted to come at all," Antoinette said. She watched the girl guardedly. She still did not know if Margaree had some specific knowledge that would be dangerous.

"I've always dreamed of Stornoway," Margaree said, which was true.

"And, I suppose, that it would someday be yours," Antoinette said. She was pleased that her bluntness had caught the girl off guard, and she laughed lightly.

"We must be honest," she said. "There were quarrels over the inheritance. I'm not such a fool that I don't realize your mother told you all about them. No doubt she insisted you were the true heir to the estate. Be that as it may, those quarrels were resolved long ago to the satisfaction of the courts, and to my satisfaction. Don't think I'm capitulating by inviting you to stay. You've always been welcome. You need never have been away, if your mother had been willing to accept my offers of hospitality. But tell me about her. You said she had passed away?"

"Yes." She had to struggle to keep from saying all the things she wanted to say. She felt sure there had never been any offers to stay. Her mother would never have left Stornoway, regardless of who was mistress, without being driven away. And if those old quarrels had been settled, they had not been to her mother's satisfaction. But she kept these thoughts to herself. Somewhere in this house was a will that would, finally, settle them. She would have to stay to find it, and for that, she had to be friendly with this icy woman before her.

They chatted for a time. It still pained Margaree to talk about her mother, but she made herself answer Antoinette's questions regarding her and the life they had lived. She did not try to make it out any different from what it had been, and it had been shabby in many ways.

"Such a pity," Antoinette said, and shook her head. She picked up some papers on the desk, signaling that the interview, as it had seemed to Margaree, was at an end.

"Now I'm afraid I must give some thought to hiring another tutor for the children," she said.

"I'd be happy to continue with the plans to teach them," Margaree said.

"Nonsense. You've hardly had time even to see the home of which you dreamed for so long. And you aren't a domestic, after all, you are a member of the family. In any event, I feel sure they won't object to a few more days of holiday."

She found at dinner that the others of the household reflected Antoinette's calm acceptance of her. She noticed that both Berthe and Ralph eyed her curiously from time to time, but they kept their curiosity tightly reined, so much so that Margaree got the impression they had been given instructions on how to behave. Marc seemed to have forgotten their unpleasant scene; he was charming and easy. Jean was not there. Margaree would have liked to ask about him, but she did not want to call attention to her interest in him.

She found herself relaxing easily into the atmosphere of the place. She listened with interest to

Berthe's idle gossip about the village below. She liked the ancient rooms with their cold stone walls; the good food and wine. Especially she enjoyed the great open fires. She stared into them and thought she was looking along deep byways of time, to the most ancient past, and she was impressed by the unchangingness, the presentness, of it. She was drunk with moods.

The following morning was all blue sky and red golden sunlight, hoar frost and chirping sparrows. When her breakfast was brought at the hour she had designated the evening before, she was already dressed and waiting for it. She had looked out upon the fields and the courtyard to be seen from her window. On the way down, she looked from the narrow window along the stairs; from here one could see the village in the morning sunlight, its roofs gleaming, its chimneys smoking. It was probably a mile or two away, but it was difficult to judge the distance with confidence, it was so open and clear between the two points. It was difficult to remember that in some places about the world the air was gray and dirty.

She had decided to spend the morning exploring. Antoinette had given her leave to do so, in a sense, when she had made reference to the fact that Margaree had hardly seen Stornoway. She had ample motives for wanting to look about. If there was a will hidden here, she would have to look to find it.

And she was sure there was a will. She had

thought this out over and over, besides discussing it so often with her mother. She had considered the other possibility, that the second will had been a figment of the old man's imagination, something he had intended to do, but had not gotten around to doing. It might even have been that he had told his daughter-in-law of his intentions, and she had misinterpreted him by thinking he spoke of something he had already done.

But her mother had seen the will. Moreover, someone else had seen it too, because the old man's signature had been witnessed. So the will could not have been a figment of her mother's imagination either.

But aside from searching for the will, she had a desire to familiarize herself with Stornoway. She wanted to know every room, every stone. She wanted to permeate herself with the atmosphere of the place.

And too, she was quite simply an avid sightseer. Even had she had no connection with this house, and nothing for which to search, she would still have been eager to explore it.

But sightseeing alone is an awkward thing; one lacks the point of reference that a guide, or even a companion, can provide. Seeing it all alone, she herself felt insubstantial in the face of its timeless reality. She began to feel as if she did not exist at all as herself, but was someone else, someone grander, someone who felt quite at home in such surroundings. She walked about here and there, glimpsing old riches, and the Margaree who had lived her life in squalor and poverty became as a dream to her, while this new fantasy became real.

There were four courtyards in all. The fourth was beyond the coach houses and the storage sheds, and connected the house proper with the so-called glass house that sat right on the cliff. She saved that for later.

The first courtyard was the one served by the entrance ramp. It was the smallest of the lot, paved with large squares of stone that were often velvety with frost in the mornings. The opposite façade rose above that pallor to silvered roofs and blue skies.

The third courtyard was the cobbled stable yard, smelling of horses and hay although there were no longer any animals kept here. Sometimes too this courtyard was full of the cheerful noises of the nearby kitchens, and sometimes the children, Anne and Louis, played here; but they made less cheerful noise than did the kitchen help.

Margaree came upon them there. Anne was reading, and Louis was coloring in a book. It occurred to her as she came toward them across the courtyard that although they had ostensibly been her reason for coming to Stornoway, she had never been introduced to them. She knew that the girl was nine, and the boy seven. They were very subdued children; they seemed to concentrate on making as little noise as possible, and Margaree found herself thinking that perhaps this was merely an early lesson that they had mastered.

They saw her coming and regarded her solemnly. She did not know if they had yet been informed that she was a relative, or whether they still thought she was their new tutor. They looked wary, but then everyone at Stornoway did.

"Good morning," she greeted them.

They said "good morning," in unison, as if they had rehearsed it.

She put a finger to her lips thoughtfully and looked from one to the other of them. "Let me see," she said. "I know one of you is named Anne, and the other Louis—but I can't guess which."

This sent them both into gales of laughter that showed plainly what an artificial thing their restraint was, and what their true natures were like. She was delighted that she had been able to break the ice so easily. Solemn faces seemed to her all wrong for youngsters.

"I'm Anne," the girl said, regaining a little composure. "And this is Louis." This struck both of them as funny all over again, and their laughter rang out.

Margaree laughed with them, and said, "I'm your cousin Margaree."

They fell silent, looking at her with wider eyes. She guessed that this was the first they had been informed of her real identity.

"We thought you were going to be our new

teacher," Anne said. Louis held one of his crayons so tightly that it broke in his hands. He seemed not to notice.

"I thought so too," Margaree said. "But that's all been changed. You see, I hadn't told anyone who I really was, until I got here."

"Was it a secret?" Louis asked. Margaree nodded. "And someone told, I bet," he said.

"Did you get spanked?" Anne asked.

"Well, not exactly," Margaree said. "But I did get scolded."

The two little heads nodded sagely. They understood this business of spanking and scoldings, and the fact that Margaree was susceptible to them as they were seemed to put her into a league with them.

"We get scolded a lot," Anne said. "You'll get used to it though."

The sincerity of this advice gave Margaree a pang. It was not right that children such as these should look upon life through such sad eyes, or should speak so matter-of-factly about punishments. They were at an age when their conversation should be about pleasant things, about fun and games and adventures.

Louis, remembering his manners suddenly, held out his coloring book toward her.

"Would you like to color a picture?" he asked.

"I should love to," she said, sitting beside him on the stone bench and leafing through the pages. "Let me see. I would love to color this horse, but I'm not sure about the color. Is pink a good color for horses, do you think? Or would this purple be better?" She held up the two crayons in question.

The children laughed at her lack of horse knowledge. "Horses are brown," Louis informed her. "Or sometimes black."

"And sometimes white," Anne added.

"Anne. Louis. I want you to come inside." Antoinette's voice was like the crack of a whip. "You are not to bother your cousin."

The children grew tense and pale. They jumped up at once.

"They aren't bothering me," Margaree said, feeling some of the anxiety the children felt in the face of this loveless authority.

"They should come in anyway," Antoinette said sternly. "They've been outside long enough for one morning. It will make them irritable and whiney."

"Well," Margaree said to the children, giving them sympathetic smiles, "it's been nice talking to you. I hope we'll be good friends."

"It was nice meeting you," each of them told her in turn, sounding altogether too formal. Anne curtsied and Louis gave her a little bow, and they scuffled off to join their grandmother, who shooed them inside. Margaree was left a bit sadder to finish her explorations. As she did so, she could not help feeling sorry for the two unfortunate children, caught up in the web of unhappiness that held the people at Stornoway together. It was small wonder that they looked so solemn and old before their times. There was no one here whose laughter and good cheer they could emulate. She promised herself that she must try to brighten their lives as best she could.

Between the first courtyard, the one of the entrance ramp, and the third, with its stables, lay the deserted main courtyard. On the north side of this was a high wall, behind which she could see trees growing. She discovered that the wall concealed a little garden, which did not look very well cared for. On the other three sides of this courtyard rose elaborate façades that reminded one of the Renaissance of Italy. Colonnades and galleries framed the perfect circle of the graveled drive. Within that was a circled lawn, and at the center of that was a well at which four stone nymphs passed the centuries supporting a carved stone canopy. Although the canopy looked delicate and airy, it must have weighed tons, and she was amused to see that they could still smile after holding it aloft for centuries. She felt disappointed to discover that the well had been covered over and was no longer in use.

To the south was the stairway of the main entrance, which was never used. The stairway began modestly enough, with a narrow arch trimmed in stone leaves and fruit. But then it rose to a triple cascade of curving steps that culminated in one broad step at the high door. She crossed the withered lawn and went up the steps, and she could not help feeling that if she tried hard enough, she could remember being there a hundred, two hundred years before.

She was embarrassed when she looked out and saw Marc in the courtyard, watching her. But he only waved and smiled, and went in.

She explored inside. Without quite putting it into thought, she was searching for something more elusive than a will. She was looking for a feeling that she belonged here. She had thought she would slip into this setting like a hand into an old glove, but she had a feeling that the house was holding her at arm's length. The more she felt this, the more fervently she tried to lay hold of it.

The wing that was lived in was a frightful mixup of the old and the new. Daily use had worn out things, and they had had to be replaced. Changes in taste and style had remodeled rooms. The paneling in the great hall predated the Revolutionary War, but the floor upstairs was only thirty years old. There was a very steep stone stairway that led from the dining room down to the kitchens and its worn concavities showed how much it had been used over the years; but wooden stairs with easier treads had been built over the old stone ones.

The bathroom was like nothing she had ever seen. The plumbing was nineteenth century. The room was huge, with a fireplace at one end, for which she had been more than a little grateful when she had bathed, and a tall linen cupboard at the other end. In the center was the enormous tub itself. It sat on a dais. It was of red veined marble, with four marble pillars that went from each corner to the ceiling. On each of the pillars were candles in gilt brackets. One bathed in oceans of hot water, by candlelight, with the fire crackling at the end of the room, while red velvet draperies at the windows shut out the world. It was the most elegant thing she had ever seen.

At lunch, Marc commented upon her explorations. "Our new cousin seemed to enjoy the great staircase," he said, speaking to his mother but with a glance in Margaree's direction.

"Have you seen Chambord?" Antoinette asked.

"No," Margaree said. She thought it unnecessary to point out the ridiculousness of that question, and Antoinette did not seem to see it for herself.

"A pity," she said. "The point will be lost on you, I fear."

"Francis I," Marc explained, when Antoinette seemed disinclined to discuss it further, "had a stairs built there, at Chambord, a great double spiral on which one person may go up and another down at the same time, without ever meeting one another. It's quite well known."

He made it an embarrassment that she had never heard of it. She said nothing, but waited, and he went on finally.

"Our ancestor thought that was wrong. He was a more social sort, perhaps. He designed here instead a stairway on which people were certain to come together, and at very close quarters. Imagine a dozen ladies in vast skirts, emerging at the top of those stairs, chatting sweetly as they descended, and then coming together in an awful crush when they reached that bottleneck of an arch. They must have waited in line to get through it. I'm sure it was very amusing."

Margaree thought personally that it would have been embarrassing rather than amusing, but she knew that her sense of humor was less sophisticated than others, and she kept this thought to herself.

"It's quite lovely to look at," she said instead.

"You should have a look at the guardroom too," he said, spearing a fresh piece of pheasant with his fork.

"In the tower?" she asked, because she thought, with her limited knowledge of such houses, that that was where a guardroom would be.

"Yes, the one in this wing of the house. Have you seen it?"

She shook her head.

"One of our ancestors—I've forgotten, but I think she was an aunt—committed suicide by jumping from the window there."

"Why did she do it?" Margaree asked.

Marc shrugged. "No one ever found out. One day she was there with some friends. The room has a bad history. Our great-great-great-grandfather was fencing with his son one day, and stumbled, driving his weapon through his son's throat. Perhaps this young lady was thinking of that. One moment she seemed quite gay. The next she had walked to the window and thrown herself out."

He paused and then said, "Maybe you shouldn't

go look at the room after all, now that I think of it. You might get bad vibrations from it."

"I don't think it shall bother me," she said. "I've never suffered that urge to fling myself from high places. And I don't fence."

"Don't you?" he asked, lifting a mocking eyebrow.

She let that taunt pass her by. But she went after lunch to examine the guardroom. It did not seem at all eerie to her. Indeed, it was one of the brighter rooms of the house, which was not to say a great deal. The windows afforded a lovely view.

She went to one of them to look out; she could not help imagining the lady who had thrown herself out. What sort of unhappiness could drive one to so desperate an act? She could imagine great unhappiness, enough even that one would stop fighting, and try to run away. But to give up life altogether was unimaginable.

She came away from the window, saddened a little. Had life at Stornoway always been so gloomy? Her mother had described it differently; but perhaps her mother's memory was colored by her desire to possess Stornoway. Perhaps she remembered it more kindly than it had been.

She left the guardroom and went to explore the other wing of the house. This was a different state of affairs from the part of the house she had been examining. It had not been used in many years, and it showed its neglect and its age. There was no hint of modernization here, and no compromise for the sake of comfort or convenience. It was interesting, but cold and unpleasant. The shadows here seemed to hover closely, threateningly. She wandered through empty, dusty rooms, moving without aim or pattern, and she felt the rooms gradually closing in upon her. She did not like this part of the house, she decided.

But when she made up her mind to leave it and return to the other, lived in wing, she realized that she had lost her way. She thought she was going back by the same route, until she came into a narrow hallway lined with closed doors, that she had not seen before. The long row of doors stretched cheerlessly down either wall. Somewhere in the distance she thought she heard voices, but when she tried to determine just where they were coming from, the sound eluded her. She went down the hall, and the rooms fell silent, as if people had been startled like crickets into noiselessness by the sound of her approach.

That, now that she had left the thought form, was what was unnerving her. She had a distinct impression that she was not alone, that someone was watching or listening nearby. She felt as if there were someone just out of sight, that if she turned quickly enough, she would see them behind her. She did turn, in fact, whirling about suddenly, but the hall was empty.

"I'm letting my imagination run away with me," she told herself. But it remained, that feeling of being watched. A board creaked somewhere nearby. Imagination or not, she had a feeling that she was not alone. There was an eerie moment of conviction, as though the presence that she felt was not physical at all, but had only intruded itself upon her mind.

"Hello, is anyone here?" she asked aloud. There was no answer. She shook her head to dislodge these thoughts, and went on.

At the end of the hall was one of those dark spirals twisting upward. Thinking that she might find her way about the next floor more easily, she started up. She had to go slowly, feeling her way.

At the landing above were two doors, one apparently leading to the second-floor hall, the other revealing more steps spiraling upward.

She saw the doors in a glance, but it was necessary to watch her step, and she looked down again. But a noise brought her eyes up. The door that led upward was swinging shut, closing itself. She stood frozen, watching it until it had slammed shut with a loud crash that echoed through the house.

There was something terrifying about that door closing itself. She had an awful urge to scream or to run. She fought it down and went toward the door. She needed to assure herself that it had only been blown shut by some breeze.

But it was locked. No, she quickly told herself, that wasn't possible. The locks were ancient, the sort that required keys to operate. There was nothing so modern here as a night latch that could lock itself upon closing.

She stood motionless before the heavy door. If the key were in the lock, on the other side, and had somehow turned itself when the door slammed, she would be able to see it merely by stooping down and putting her eye to the keyhole.

She remained standing. She tried the knob again. It turned all right, just the way a knob should turn; but the door remained firmly shut—not as if it were locked, after all, but more as if someone was holding it shut from the other side.

"It's stuck," she told herself firmly. "Doors do stick, and if I put my shoulder to it, and pushed hard it would open."

Instead, she took her hand away from the knob, and held her breath, listening. Surely she was imagining things. That couldn't be the sound of breathing from the other side of the door, no matter how much it sounded like it. There was no doubt an open window above, and for some reason curtains hanging at it, and the wind was blowing the curtains, just as it had blown the door closed, and the curtains were wispy things that sounded, when they rustled, like someone breathing hoarsely. And she had been wandering about in this old house by herself, letting her imagination run away with her, for too long it seemed.

There was surely no one on the other side of the door, because no one had a reason to hide from her, or to try to frighten her.

She decided that she did not want to see where the stairs led anyway. She turned toward the other door, that led to the second-floor hall. A sound startled her, and made her look back.

The knob of the closed door was turning. It was turning slowly, hesitantly—but it was unmistakably turning.

Her skin crawled. She had an unaccountable sensation of fear. Yet she could not move or speak; she could only stare with wide, fascinated eyes at that ancient brass knob slowly twisting.

"Mademoiselle. Je vous en prie."

The woman, a servant Margaree had not seen heretofore, appeared so suddenly from the hall that Margaree jumped a foot. The woman was nearly as surprised to see her, and plainly unhappy about it. She unleashed a loud stream of chatter in French, a local dialect that was incomprehensible to Margaree. All the while, she had a firm hold on Margaree's wrist, and was tugging her away from the stairs, into the hall.

"I can't understand you," Margaree said sharply, because she had been frightened and annoyed at being dragged about so roughly.

The French went on in a rush. Berthe appeared down the hall, hurrying along toward them.

"What are you doing here?" she demanded breathlessly of Margaree. She too looked frightened and angry.

The woman in the maid's uniform let go of Margaree's hand, but she had moved to put herself between Margaree and the stairs landing, as if she thought Margaree might make a run for it.

"I was just exploring," Margaree said. She was meek at first, but her anger, now that she had gotten over her fear, made her voice rise quickly. "And I don't like being shoved about like a piece of baggage. There was someone up those stairs, hiding behind a closed door, which I think is odd. And then this woman set upon me as if I were a thief."

"You're not supposed to be here," Berthe said, her red face redder still with her haste and her excitement.

Antoinette spoke from behind Margaree, from the stairs. "Please," she said, her calm voice in sharp contrast to their excited ones. "You are yelling."

Margaree felt embarrassed at having been caught in this shabby little scene. It would not add favorably to the impression she was creating of herself in Antoinette's eyes.

"I'm sorry," she said contritely. "But I . . ."

"Yes, I heard," Antoinette said. "You heard someone. You were exploring. This"—she waved her hand toward the stairs and upward—"is where my husband keeps his apartments. We try not to disturb him here. I should have warned you."

Margaree stood in silence for a moment. There were a number of things she would have liked to say and ask. But the silly scene in which Antoinette had found her had left her on the wrong footing. She had to remember why she was here, and what she wanted to accomplish.

"I'm sorry," she said. "I didn't know this part of the house was forbidden."

"It's all right," Antoinette said.

An awkward silence followed. They all seemed to be watching her and waiting for her to leave, Margaree thought. She could think of no justification for staying, but she was ashamed to have to say, "I've gotten turned around. I don't know how to get back." She felt stupid as well as vulgar.

"This hall will take you to the main hall," Antoinette said, adding with what may or may not have been a touch of sarcasm, "Can you find your way from there?"

Margaree assured her that she could and left, aware as she walked the length of the hall that they remained where they were watching her. She did not look back, but she knew this was so.

As she went by empty rooms, watching dust motes dance in the air before her, she wondered why her Uncle Yves would live in this empty shell, amid empty rooms and dust. Why had he hidden behind a closed door, if that had been him on the other side of the door?

CHAPTER 7

Jean Copley was restless. Most of the time, when he was not fighting with his family, especially Marc whom he strongly disliked, he was a man at peace with himself. He had almost no roots, except to the island itself, and he sometimes thought of the entire island of Cape Breton as his home. He had his boat, which was his home more of the time than even he realized. For the rest, he sometimes had a room at the inn. The widow who ran it always saw that there was a place for him to lay his handsome head. And occasionally he stayed up at the house—almost never in the house proper, but in the glass house. It had been the old man's favorite place, and he and the old man had come to be friends in the relatively short time they had known each other. Since no one else used the glass house, he could regard it more or less as his own, and he rather liked having it to come back to.

It had never occurred to him before that his life was lonely. He had been content to spend his time largely in his own company, or in the company of the local fishermen, who had long since stopped thinking of him as one of the Harrod family and treated him now as an equal. If he needed something more than that, there had been the pink-faced widow who was prettier by night than she appeared by day.

But something was amiss now. He had rambled restlessly from boat to widow to glass house, and back to the inn, and he could not escape the feeling of something missing. He caught himself listening, as if for someone's approach, or the sound of a particular voice. He seemed to be waiting, except there was nothing for him to be waiting for.

He sat in the noisy taproom and drank an ale and tried to stop watching the door from the street for an unknown someone to enter.

"Hey, Jean, how about a game of darts," one of the other fishermen called to him. "I could use a little of your money."

"Playing with you is like stealing," he called back. He drained his stein and got up from his stool.

"Will you be staying the night?" the widow asked from across the bar. She had a soft Scottish burr that he liked well enough.

"We'll see," he said evasively, and went out into

the noontime light. He went out of town with a long-legged stride, toward the house. He did not take the road, but followed the path that cut up the hill at a steep slant. He had not seen the girl—Margaree, it was a pretty, Cape Breton name—since she'd revealed who she was. He hadn't gone back for dinner that day, or at all the next day. He wasn't in the habit of spending his time with the family anyway, and when he was around this girl, he had a strange trapped feeling, as if his freedom were being subtly tugged out of his hands. He had thought about her, and decided that he knew the type of girl well enough. She wasn't the type you could just have a tumble with, and she wasn't the type you could just have for a friend. Those great wide eyes of hers saw things too seriously, and from one point of view only. If a man wanted her, there was just one way he could have her.

Well, she'd settled those eyes on the wrong one this time. He wasn't a marrying man, and he meant to have that clear between them from the first. He had made up his mind that he would avoid seeing her, and when he did, he would be cool until she got the picture.

So that was that.

He came over the top of the hill, and saw her coming toward him, crossing the courtyard that separated the glass house from the big house. She was wearing a skirt and sweater and she moved with an unconscious grace that made his throat go dry. She looked up and saw him; her pretty face broke into a smile and she waved. Without thinking, he grinned and waved back.

Their paths came together in the middle of the courtyard. She looked shy, but happy to see him.

"I wondered if you had gone away," she said.

"I don't come up to the house much. The Harrods and me don't get along."

She did not see fit to point out that his mother was a Harrod, and that she was one too. She thought she knew who and what he meant. She tried to think of something else to say, something bright and poised and clever. Nothing crossed her mind that seemed right, and the moment grew painfully long.

"Have you seen the glass house?" he asked.

"No, I was just going."

"Come on then." He practised none of his stepbrother's bowing and scraping. He simply turned and started off toward the glass house, on the assumption that she would follow.

She did, and when he began to tell her about the cottage, she did not point out that she had known its history from childhood, or that had justice been done, she and her mother might have lived here in the past. She listened attentively, and observed that he seemed to care far more for the cottage than he did for the house.

There was a certain justification for that attitude. It was a lovely home, a "cottage" only by virtue of being attached to that great mansion. There was a large front room, which was actually at the back, so that the view was over the cliffs and the rolling ocean.

"They call it the glass house," he said, flinging open one of the big French windows that lined one entire wall, "because of these windows. It was pretty uncommon to have a whole wall of glass like this, especially here, with the storms we get up here. That door just around the corner is storage for the shutters. They have to go up whenever it starts blowing, or the whole house would be flooded in no time."

"It was worth it, though," she said, standing by him at the window. "I don't think I've ever seen a view as lovely as this. You'd think Stornoway would have been built to take better advantage of the view."

It was his favorite view, this sweeping vista of rock and sea before them. He had never shared it with anyone before, since the old man had died. He shot Margaree a sideways glance. She was peculiar. Fuss over a room that was perfectly comfortable because it was too small, and then make over a view. It irritated him that he couldn't fit her into any of the molds he had created for pigeonholing people.

"I expect they took the ocean for granted," he said gruffly, and turned away.

She followed him through the rest of the house, wondering what she could possibly have said that would have annoyed him.

One of the bedrooms had a lived-in look. A

man's clothes were scattered about, none too neatly. A pair of muddy boots had been set to dry without thought for the expensive carpeting that they had since stained irreparably.

"Someone's living here," she said, surprised. She had gotten the impression that the cottage was unused.

"I stay here part of the time," he said. He looked around, trying to see the room with her eyes, and succeeded in seeing that it looked messy. He thought it unfair of her to come in uninvited and disapprove of the way he lived his life.

"That's all there is to see," he said, and ushered her outside in an authoritative way.

Outside, though, he was in no hurry to part. "The old man liked the cottage best," he said. "He used to come here a lot, especially to watch the sunset."

"Did you come with him?" she asked. His tone, when he spoke of "the old man," was one of affectionate respect, far different from what he used when he spoke of the others of the family.

"Sometimes," he said. The conversation waned for a moment. "I've got a boat," he said finally, apropos of nothing. "I'm going down there now."

He waited for another moment or two of silence, but she did not pick up on this hint, to his annoyance. "Well," he said, turning his back on her, "I'm going."

"May I come with you?" she asked.

His back was turned, so that she heard his reply,

"If you want," but did not see the little-boy grin that turned the corners of his mouth briefly upward.

He led the way down the path, slowing his pace to accommodate hers, and giving her his hand to help her over some of the difficult spots.

They were the object of curious stares as they passed through the town. Both of them ignored the stares, for their own reasons. She could not help but observe that more than a few of the young women of the town looked envious, and she knew without being told that he was looked upon as "a catch." Because she was a woman, and with him, she was pleased.

At the wharf they passed a group of young men standing by a piling. He knew them, and they knew him. He saw the looks they gave her, and knew what they were thinking. He swept a look over the group that effectively stifled the remarks they might have made otherwise, and there was only silence as he and Margaree walked by.

The boat was small; to her surprise, after the disarray of his bedroom at the glass house, it was immaculately clean. The sail was as white as snow, the decks looked freshly scrubbed. A mat covered in ducking had been spread across the bow, and he invited her to sit there while he took them out of the little harbor, following the cliffs out to sea. They spoke very little. It seemed unnecessary.

She watched him while he worked with sail and tiller. He seemed a different man here on the water.

He looked at home, confident and at ease; he had left that gruff awkwardness behind on the dock.

He stripped off his shirt, not even thinking to ask if she minded. She watched the play of the noon sun upon his bronze skin. He looked like a sea god, bent to the wheel, muscles rippling. Something that was new to her and vaguely disquieting stirred within her. She looked away.

When they were out a ways, he said, "Come here."

She came to stand by him. He pointed up, and above them, on the cliff, she saw the glass house, its windows reflecting the sunlight like so many brilliant gems. She realized why it was an object of such wonder to the local people. There was nothing like it anywhere around.

"It's lovely," she said. She seemed to be seeing two scenes at once, like a double exposure on a film. She saw the view from here, looking up at the cottage, and superimposed over it was the view as she had seen it from there a short time before, as if she were looking down upon herself in this boat. "I think I would rather live there, in the cottage. It's warmer than Stornoway."

"Don't you like the big house?"

She lifted her shoulders and let them fall. "I don't know. I think not, and yet it's in my blood. I'm obsessed by it perhaps."

"I don't understand you," he said softly. "What do you want? Do you want to be a part of that family? They aren't worth getting yourself worked up over."

"I want Stornoway," she said. She said it automatically, because she had been saying it so often, for so long a time.

He looked disappointed though, and for a moment concentrated on the wheel. But they were out from the land now, and the boat did not really need the attention.

"You should be happy, then," he said.

"Why do you say that?"

"You're there, aren't you, at Stornoway. Isn't that what you want, to be at Stornoway?"

"I want to own it," she said.

"Now you sound like a Harrod," he said sharply.

Her eyes flashed. "I am a Harrod," she said, every bit as sharp as he had been.

He made a sound like a grunt, and yanked hard at the wheel, so that the boat heeled sharply, and the glass house swung out of view.

She went angrily back to the bow, kneeling on the mat and watching the roll of waves. She put into words in her mind the criticism that he had only implied, and resented him for it. She knew that her answer had sounded greedy and grasping, but he did not know all that was behind it. He did not know of the years of poverty, living from hand to mouth, and all the time knowing that she should be living in wealth. He did not know what a taste of bitter resentment that could leave in the mouth.

He did not know of her mother's lifetime of unhappiness, that had affected her too. He did not know what it was to realize of someone you loved that every day of her life was a time for mourning. He did not know of the promise she had given her mother on her deathbed.

She was even angry because he did not know, without being told, of these things.

He too was angry, angry because he did not want her to be like the Harrods, not even a little bit; angry with himself because he did not know why it mattered.

He let the wheel go. They were in open water now and it didn't matter much if they drifted. He stared at the angry set of her shoulders, her rigid back turned to him. She gleamed in the same golden way that the sunlight did on the crests of the waves.

Something entirely strange burned within him. It was anger in part, but not at all like the anger he felt towards, say, his family. It was desire in part, but not at all like the desire he had felt, and expressed, toward other women. It was a tenderness, in fact, that belied those other two feelings.

Without thinking of what he was doing, he went swiftly to her. Stooping, he turned her toward him and pulling her into his arms, he kissed her.

She had not heard him approaching across the boat. One moment she was alone, angrily watching the sea, and the next she was in his arms, crushed against his naked, massive chest. The scent of him, of sea and sweat and something that she could not identify but that was desire for her, filled her nostrils, overwhelming her. She had never been in a man's arms like this. Her lips had never been covered like this with other lips. She had read romantic novels, and contemplated the desires and passions that often burned within those fictional women. She had never dreamed that such desires and passions might exist within her as well.

But they did, they did!

She sank back upon the rough mat, not with any conscious design, but because all power of rigidity seemed to have fled her body, leaving it fluid and yielding, as his was firm and demanding. For a moment she saw the dark cloud of his hair framed by the brilliant blue of the sky, seeming even to reflect it. Then he blotted the sun and the sky from her sight, and his lips sought hers again, and this time it was he who was surprised.

Never in her wildest imaginings, had she dreamed all that was meant by that inadequate phrase, making love.

Now she knew.

CHAPTER 8

The sky was gray and salmon colored when he helped her onto the wharf. All of his anger and gruffness seemed to have been taken from him, and he was gentleness itself.

"I ought to get back," she said when he led her away from the house on the hill.

"You've missed dinner," he said. "We may as well eat at the inn. Besides, I'm in no hurry to take you back there."

She could not argue with that, and she came along with him happily. Several times as they walked he glanced over at her, but it was no longer in the doubtful, suspicious way he had looked at her before. Rather he seemed dazed by something, and wondering. But whenever she looked back at him, he smiled and seemed satisfied with what he had seen.

Her heart sang. She understood now why she had never truly felt anything for a man before. She had been waiting. Without knowing it, she had waited for him and this time. She was complete. She was in love.

They came to the inn. He had told her that he sometimes stayed here, and usually ate here, and she was curious to see the place. She looked eagerly around the long rustic room that he ushered her into; a man's room, with warm fires and open beams, and dirt on the floors. Behind the bar was a plump barmaid who seemed to take quite an interest in them. Margaree saw the looks the girl was giving Jean, and wondered if she sometimes provided for his other appetites as well. But she did not ask, and pretended not to notice when the girl set things down on their table so hard that the glasses rattled.

He took it for granted that he was to order for her, and she did not object or question. She drank an ale with him, which tasted delicious after the sea air, and gazed at him fondly. The long silences that fell between them now were comfortable and unstrained. Before it had seemed at times as if they had no words for one another; now, they needed none.

The food he had ordered came. The sullen-looking serving girl set a plate before her that held what looked like small scallops, flattened and fried. The flavor was rich yet delicate; she had to ask what they were.

"Fried cod tongues," he told her, amused by her ignorance. They were, she learned, a delicacy, that must be eaten the same day the fish are caught if they are not to turn tough and glutinous.

With them was a dish of the fiddleheads, the young still unfurling fronds of the ostrich fern, cooked and enhanced with a lump of melting butter. Dessert was a steamed cranberry pudding. It was a simpler meal than what they had at Stornoway, but infinitely better.

"What kind of fishing do you do, anyway?" she asked.

"Cod, in the past," he said. "But I'm switching over to crab. That's still new here."

"I had an idea crabs came from the northwest," she said.

"They do, the king crab. Nobody knew the queen crab existed until recently. But there they were, all the time, three hundred and more feet down in the gulf, just waiting to be found and eaten."

He talked with more animation than was usual for him, of the accidental discovery of the queen crab, smaller and more succulent than the king. New traps had been created, similar to lobster pots, for catching them in quantities. He himself had designed a new trap of steel and nylon that seemed to work better than any other.

"That's why I was fighting with my mother for money, to make the new traps and finance a season working the gulf. It wasn't like I was asking any favors. I pay my own way, unlike the rest of the family. And I only wanted a loan. I could pay it back after one season, and still live like a rich man."

"But you could live like a rich man without that effort," she said.

"I wouldn't live at Stornoway," he said sharply. They were silent for a minute. Then he said, looking up at her through his thick lashes, "But if I was to settle down with someone, I would want to live in the glass house. It would be a good place to live with the right woman, the one you want to come home to at night."

She could think of nothing to say but, "That would be nice."

He seemed suddenly embarrassed again by that impulsive declaration, and the conversation dwindled. The woman from behind the bar brought their bill, and he paid.

"Been out fishing?" she asked, hand on hip while she waited for his money.

"Could be," he replied, ignoring the saucy look she gave him.

"Catch anything?" she asked. She laughed, and one of the men in the room laughed too, but a quick, hard look from Jean silenced him. Margaree blushed.

"Hey, Liz," one of the customers called after the barmaid, "how about letting me come into the kitchen with you?"

"Come ahead," she called in a flirtatious voice, "if you think you can stir anything up."

He followed her through the swinging door into the kitchen, to the accompaniment of laughter and catcalls from his cronies.

"Let's go," Jean said, standing. They went out hand in hand.

In the kitchen Liz, the widow, heard the door close after them; something wrenched at her heart.

"How about that kiss you've been promising me?" the man with her asked, trying to get his great arms about her.

"Get out of here with you," she said angrily, giving him a shove.

"What's got into you?" he asked, astonished by the sudden change in her manner. A moment before she had been all laughs and teasing, and now, just like that, she looked like she was going to cry.

She lost her temper then. "Out," she said, smacking him atop the head with a wooden spoon. "Out of my kitchen with your foolishness."

He went, shaking his head, to sit again with his cronies and remark upon the unfathomable behavior of women as opposed to the sea; a man could understand the sea.

He took her up by the road rather than the path, because it was night now, and he was afraid she might stumble on the steep path. Stornoway loomed above them as they walked, its lighted windows like so many eyes watching them.

"Why is my Uncle Yves living in the unused wing of the house?" she asked impulsively. She had forgotten until now that the man with her was a Harrod, who could answer many of her questions about the house.

"He's crazy," Jean said simply.

Margaree stopped abruptly. "Crazy? You mean really insane?"

"Yes." He seemed to find nothing striking in the fact. "They say it was drugs. He used to take a lot of different things, I remember that. Half the time he was like he was dead drunk, or worse. It was like he was trying to escape from something. And he was a slave to my mother, he was obsessed with keeping her happy. One time one of the maids did something that made my mother angry. That night, Yves attacked the girl, and would have killed her if some men hadn't heard her screaming and come along. After that, some people in town tried to make her put him away in an asylum, but she would not hear of it. She said he was hers, and he would stay at Stornoway, and she would see that he didn't do any harm. She's pretty strong about looking after her own. Anyway, she started locking him up whenever he was having one of his spells, which wasn't very often, and everybody seemed satisfied with that. Most people have forgotten he's still up there."

"Is he dangerous?" she asked.

"I don't suppose so, ordinarily. He has times when he is, but most of the time he just sits and daydreams."

After a pause, she said, "Someone has been coming to my room at night."

"Who?"

"I don't know. Sometimes they open the door a crack, and sometimes not."

"You think it's him?"

"I don't know. It's someone. I thought at first I might be dreaming it, but it's no dream."

They went on toward the house. He was thoughtful for a bit.

"He's supposed to be locked up if it looks like one of those spells is coming on," he said. "And like I say, even if he is wandering at night, he isn't likely to be dangerous. But I'll check on it anyway. You ought to keep your door locked, just to be safe."

"There's no lock on my door," she said.

They had reached the gate into the small courtyard that was used for the entrance. He stopped, taking hold of her hands.

"I'll look into that too," he said. "Anyway, it can't matter much. You aren't going to be there that long. And no one will ever trouble us in the glass house. There aren't any locks on those doors either, but no one will bother us."

There was another of those long pauses. She asked, "Are you talking about getting married?"

"Of course," he said with a chuckle. "Did you think I was just having fun?"

The cloud that had been lingering in front of the moon suddenly scurried on, remembering some errand elsewhere. The moonlight fell full upon her face. He stopped laughing.

"Isn't that what you wanted?" he asked. His breath was tight in his throat.

"I don't know," she said, too quickly, without thinking before she said it. She saw something change all at once in his face, as if a door had suddenly slammed shut on something.

"Oh, of course it is," she said, grabbing for the hand he had taken from her. "You've made me very happy. But it doesn't have to be at once, does it?"

"Why would we wait?" he asked.

"Because of Stornoway, and all that unsettled business," she said. "I need time to get that straightened away first."

He smiled, but it was not the tender expression he had been bestowing upon her through the afternoon, not the smile he had given her lying on the deck of the boat in the warm sunlight.

"Yes, I see," he said.

She saw that he did not see. "I told you about my mother," she said, pleading for understanding. "And the promise I made her. I have to keep that. Don't you understand?"

"I understand Stornoway," he said. "And the Harrods." He was angry. He felt he had somehow been deceived and cheated, tricked into exposing all of his secrets.

"If you loved me . . ." she began.

He cut her short with an angry laugh. "Love

you? I'm a fisherman. I love the sea. And if I need a woman, there's one in town waiting for me. And I'm going to her now. Good night, Miss Harrod."

He turned on his heel and went quickly down the drive, into the night.

She wanted to cry his name, and run after him. But the stubborn pride and icy reserve that had so often prevented her from showing her feelings held her in check now. And she too was angry. He ought to have understood why this was important to her. It wasn't merely greed. Once she had Stornoway, she would happily give it away, to prove how little she cared for that sort of wealth.

But she had to have it, to set things right.

She sighed and turned to go into the house. He would just have to come to understand. If not before, then after. She would indeed give Stornoway away if need be.

She smiled ruefully at herself. Already she was giving the house away, and thus far she had made no progress at all in proving that it was hers.

Where was that will? She knew it existed, somewhere. Her mother had seen it herself, and the old man had told her he had hidden it where it would be safe until he could have it put in the proper place. He had had a safe deposit box, and had meant on his next trip to town to put the will in it; but death had intervened, and the will's hiding place had remained the old man's secret.

Stornoway. There were a thousand and one places where a will might be hidden. And she could not go through the house room by room tearing it apart. She thought Antoinette did not know that she knew of the will. If Antoinette learned that, and saw that she was searching for it, she would most certainly intervene. Her search had to be done in secret, which only made it infinitely harder.

She went in through the door, into the house, feeling all at once discouraged. How could she hope to find the document for which she was searching? Others far cleverer than she had searched freely and thoroughly, with no success.

The family was in the drawing room, having coffee. She thought that she ought to offer an explanation for her absence, and it was the easiest to tell the truth.

"I was with Jean," she said. Antoinette did not show any particular response to this; Marc smirked in a way that annoyed Margaree.

She stayed long enough to be polite and then, excusing herself, started to her own room. She took the spiral staircase in the rear. At its base, she paused. The hanging lights were not burning, and the stairs were completely dark. Something about that darkness seemed to her ominous and threatening.

"You've got to stop shaking every time you see a shadow," she told herself. She made herself start up.

The stairs were worn badly. That and their dizzying spiral made them hard to negotiate even with light. She tripped halfway up. She had been feeling her way with her hands against the rough stone, but as she fell, she reached out for the iron railing, grabbing at it.

Instead of the solid support that she expected from it, it came loose with a ripping sound. The entire metal structure came away under the force of her fall. She screamed, crashing down upon the worn stone, her upper body dangling in air over the edge of the steps. The long metal railing fell to the floor far below with a deafening crash. If she had had a better grip on it, it might have carried her with it, and she would be lying now among that broken heap of twisted metal below.

She lay half on, half off the steps, breathing hard. Below there was a clatter of running footsteps.

"What on earth . . ." Marc cried. The others came in his wake, Berthe and Ralph and finally, not hurrying, Antoinette.

"What happened?" Marc demanded, helping her to her feet. She was grateful for the feel of his arms just then.

"The railing broke away," she said a bit shakily. "I stumbled in the dark and grabbed for it, and it just tore loose."

"I came up these stairs just a couple of hours ago," he said. "I didn't see anything wrong with the railing then."

"This old house," Berthe said, and gave her head a disapproving shake.

"You'd better have all the stairs checked in the morning," Antoinette said. "That is most dangerous. Your cousin might have been killed."

Something in the timber of her voice made Margaree shiver as if a cold wind had blown across her. She looked at the faces around her and thought, *Yes, and none of you would mind.*

And why should they? Even without the will, she was a threat to them, another heir who could at the very least claim a part of what they had heretofore regarded as theirs. And Antoinette, despite her calm confidence, might still be afraid of that other will.

Everyone of them, Margaree thought, has reason to want me dead.

CHAPTER 9

Antoinette watched her scurry up the stairs, looking like a frightened churchmouse.

Good, she thought, let her be frightened. And this is only the beginning.

"Have someone clean this up," she said to Marc, indicating the debris on the floor. She went disdainfully up to her own room.

She was not at all happy with Margaree's presence in the house. It had been necessary to keep her here, of course, to see what if anything she knew. It was always best to keep one's enemies close at hand. What was it the Orientals said: in order to stab a man in the back, one must stand very close to him. Better to keep that girl here where she could keep a close eye on her.

Still, there was something about the way the girl had attached herself to Stornoway. Already she was looking and acting as if the house was hers. Antoinette knew that sort of possessive love; she had felt it herself when first she had seen Stornoway, and had known that she must make the house her own.

Not that this girl was as strong or determined as she. But there was a stubborn streak in her that would not let an idea die easily.

And now this business with Jean. She had never counted on that. Anyone else she could have managed—but Jean. He was impossible to control. And if this girl got her claws into him, and persuaded him to her way of thinking . . . Jean would never rest until he had accomplished anything that he set out to do. He'd gotten that from his mother, and it gave her a certain sense of pride at the same time that it angered her.

Dressed in a silk gown, she slipped into her bed. The light that was never out burned on the stand. But she could not sleep. She had a sixth sense about these things, and she knew that trouble was brewing. She would have to be doubly alert if she were to manage.

She sighed. Well, there was always a way. She had no scruples to put a limit on how far she might go. Miss Margaree Butler Harrod would be managed, one way or the other. Dead women inherited nothing but the grave.

It did not even surprise her that she should contemplate anything so drastic. She had always done whatever needed to be done to accomplish her end.

Her logic was simple. What she wanted was right. And in achieving right, the end justified the means. She had not hesitated to make a slave of her own husband. She had not made him weak. She had not started him on drugs. She had only taken advantage of the opportunities he gave her, encouraging him in his addictions, providing new things for him, but only because he asked her to.

And what harm had she done? He had been miserable before, unable to cope with the world in which he found himself. He was too small a man to face life on its own terms. She had only helped him find the terms with which he could cope. He was vastly happier now, with no need to think for himself, nothing to concern him but eating and sleeping and pleasing her in little ways. He was happy in the diminished world in which he now lived. Other men found their happiness with women, or in a bottle, or in business careers, or travel. What was wrong with each man living as he was best suited to live? Yves had been born to be a fool. It would have been real madness for him to try to live out his life any other way.

She sighed, bringing her thoughts back from this path to the one that was most important just now.

Yes, perhaps that would be the best solution with the girl. But she must think about it, and how it could be best managed. There must be no risk in it. An accident, perhaps. Or Yves. She had been planting the seeds already for that possibility. She was always prepared. That was what made her so much more successful than others. Whatever needed to be done, she was always ready to do it when the time came.

Margaree searched, with no success. Everywhere she looked, she seemed to see another possible hiding place, but each one in turn seemed too obvious. It was useless to look behind hanging pictures and under furniture. Anything hidden in that manner would have been found long ago.

"And anything hidden really well," she told herself with a sense of frustration, "you can't risk looking for without getting caught."

She had awakened in a despondent mood. Everything had gone wrong. The disagreement with Jean had taken on size and weight overnight. She saw how strongly he felt about the family, and about Stornoway. They could not help but clash on the question of her inheritance. Disdaining the place as he did, he was not likely to ever understand why it should matter to her.

She was haunted too by the thought that the people with whom she was living—her family, as it were—might all be happy to see her die. It was ironic. She had wondered about them for most of her life, resented, and at the same time yearned for them, wanting to undo the rejection that had been her heritage. And now they were suddenly a source of fear, because she saw that it was only a small step from being happy to see someone dead, to wish them dead, to do something about it.

That thought, when it had first come to her in the gloom of the stairs, had seemed ridiculous. "People don't do that sort of thing except in novels," she had told herself in the stillness of her room.

But people *did* do that sort of thing, one could hardly read the newspapers without knowing that, and often for far less reason than a large inheritance.

She had come up and down those stairs a dozen times already, and always that railing had seemed perfectly safe and sound. How had it come loose so suddenly? She had looked at it by the light of morning, but her ignorant eye could see nothing to tell her if it had been tampered with.

Why had the lights there been out, when usually they burned all night? Had someone meant her not to see that the railing had been loosened? Had someone known that she almost certainly must trip in the darkness on those steep, spiraling stairs?

She did not want these thoughts; she tried to dispel them from her mind. But they came unbidden, and refused to be put out, and she could not help but dwell upon them.

An idea had come to her during the night. Jean had said that the glass house was her grandfather's favorite place and that he had gone there often to be alone, or with the young Jean to watch the sunset. The idea had come to her that perhaps it was there, in the glass house, that he had hidden the will.

A search there revealed nothing, however. She did not search the bedroom that Jean used. Something about that idea seemed wrong to her. She stood in the doorway instead, and wondered why he had picked things up so neatly. There was no sign of scattered clothes or dirty boots. The room had an unoccupied look.

She went back to the living room, and went to stand at the French windows overlooking the sea. Only a short distance away was a wooden landing and the beginning of steps that, Jean had told her, led to the Harrods' own private cove by the water. It was too close below for her to see that, of course. Out on the water she saw the white triangle of a sail, and wondered if it were Jean in his fishing boat. Perhaps even now he was looking up at the reflections of the windows, thinking of her. In her mind's eye, she saw him shirtless, his powerful manly body gleaming with sweat and sun. She remembered the feel of his arms about her, his lips on hers.

"This is ridiculous," she said aloud. "I've got to patch things up with him."

She went out, determined that she would go down to the village to look for him, and try to end their quarrel. But as she came across the main courtyard, she saw Marc. He saw her at about the same time and veered toward her. Their paths crossed near the old well.

"And here," he said, imitating a tour guide delivering a lecture, "the central court of Stornoway. Here the first of the Harrods drank water and said that it was better than any wine he had ever had. And here, centuries later, a man met a beautiful young lady, braving the cold for a drink at that great well."

It was colder; the sky was crowded with purplish heavy clouds.

"Or did you have some other errand?" he asked.

"No," she said, because she could not tell him what she had been going to do. "I was only out walking. I couldn't drink from this anyway, though. It's covered. Is it dry?"

"No, not dry." He studied the well with its canopy held aloft by stone nymphs. "One of our ancestors—let me see, a great great uncle, I think, but I'm bad with history. At any rate, he disappeared one day. A month or so later, someone found him bobbing about in the well. They fished him out all right, but they couldn't make up their minds if he had killed himself or been pushed in. It seems there was a member of the family then as strong willed as my mother."

He smiled when he said this, but she had an odd feeling that he meant more to inform than to amuse. She said nothing.

"The general feeling after a time was that he had been pushed, to settle some squabble over the estate. So the family did the only sensible thing, they punished the well, by covering it over."

He thumped on the old wood. Something fell within, and after a lengthy silence, a faint splash echoed from below.

"Mind you," he said, shrugging, "that's the story as I heard it. The truth may have been that the water level got too low, and it was easier to use the other wells. There are three others. Someone drowned in the one in the kitchen too, but there was never any talk of covering it over. The water from that one is the best around, and everyone thought it would be too much of a shame to cover it. I think this is Arethusa." He put a finger to the nose of one stone nymph.

"Did my story frighten you?" he asked.

"Was it meant to?" she asked in reply.

"You misjudge me," he said.

"I did at first."

"Marc, I want to see you." It was Antoinette's voice, from the open doorway of the house. She did not call any greeting to Margaree, although she nodded in reply to Margaree's greeting.

It seemed to Margaree that Antoinette was always there, appearing in an arch or doorway, whenever she became engaged in conversation with someone. If it weren't so incredible, she would suspect the older woman of being jealous of her. But that, she knew, was ridiculous.

"Enjoy your stroll," Marc said, and hastened to his mother's side. They went in.

It did not seem to bother him in the least that his mother treated him in a servile way. It is a mistake,

Margaree thought, to believe that another person should automatically resent being dominated. She would resent it, and probably most people would. But that did not make it a law of nature that everyone would. To some, that domination might be a sort of security. By bending themselves to another's will, they absolved themselves of responsibility. It was so in any business organization. Most people had ambition, desiring and working toward better jobs with more pay and more responsibility. But there was always that workhorse who was perfectly content to be where she was, and truly did not want to be a chief.

Marc was like that, and although he was rich and handsome and had charm, she pitied the poor girl who eventually married him, particularly when Antoinette died.

Or, more likely, she thought, walking back to the house herself, he would marry when Antoinette had died, and he would choose a girl like Antoinette, to dominate and decide for him, and allow him a certain amount of schoolboy freedom.

She had meant to go in search of Jean before lunch, but when she came in she saw the children reading quietly in the library and she put aside her own problems in the face of their all too obvious loneliness.

They looked more than happy to see her, and she was reminded again that no one in this house seemed to notice them except to disapprove of them in some way.

She saw that Anne was reading a history book, and Louis a volume of the encyclopedia. She felt certain that these could not have been their own choices, and asked, "Isn't there anything on the shelves here you'd rather be reading?"

"We aren't allowed to take books off the shelves," Anne explained. "We have to ask for them. These were the ones mother pulled for us."

Margaree could well imagine Berthe, impatient and disinterested, grabbing these two volumes at random without any real thought for the children's interest.

"Well," she said aloud, "no one's told me I couldn't take books down. Let's see what we can find."

She looked over the titles on the shelves. Both of the children followed her closely, and their eagerness told her that they did indeed have an interest in books, if something could be found a little more to their tastes.

The books on the shelves had not been selected with young children in mind, and for a time she could sympathize a little with Berthe's problem in finding something of interest to them. But at last she came upon a translation in English of the *Chanson de Roland*. She glanced through it and saw that it was not a literal translation, but rather a free retelling of those heroic tales. She rather thought that the children would be as fascinated by those valiant knights and fair ladies as she had been.

With their help she rearranged the chairs, so that

one could sit on either side of her. They fell into rapt silence when she began to read.

The saga was already known to her, yet she found herself absorbed in it once again as she read. She shared the excitement of her young audience when the knights of Roland's small force were trapped in the narrow winding gorge of the Pyrénées. She thrilled when Roland refused to sound his great horn to bring the aid of Charlemagne. And at last, when nearly all were dead, the horn was sounded, and Charlemagne came swiftly, "his white beard flying in the wind." But the way was long, "high are the mountains, vast and dark; deep are the valleys, swift the streams."

The children listened entranced as Roland mourned the death of his beloved friend, Oliver, and at last, mortally wounded, with his last strength, he broke his jeweled sword Durendal, lest it should fall into heathen hands.

And when Roland, remembering sweet France, his family, Charlemagne whom he loved, wept, Louis on his chair beside Margaree emitted a succession of sniffles that said more plainly than any words how much he had enjoyed the story.

It was lunchtime when she had finished, and she sent the children off, pleased by their heartfelt expressions of gratitude. She wished that she could have lunch with them, which she now knew they took in the kitchen, than with the gloomy adults of the Harrod family. But she knew it was pointless to ask; Antoinette would never agree to anything so unseemly.

She had lunch after all in the dining room. When she came up to her room afterward, she found one of the servants installing a bolt on her door, "on instructions," he explained.

There was a note from Jean as well:

I've moved my things out of the glass house. No one will object if you want to move in there. You'll be safe there.

The suggestion that she was unsafe in the big house echoed her own thoughts so ominously that it added to her feeling of uneasiness. She recalled that she had said she would like to live in the glass house; at the time it had been only an idle comment. Later, when he had suggested they might live there together, she had been more serious. But certainly she had never meant that he should give up his room there and move out so that she could move in. Now she would have to see him, to resolve this misunderstanding.

She found him in the inn. Her entrance created a little flurry of interest, and she knew that many of the eyes in the room were watching as she walked up to the wooden table at which Jean was seated. He did not look altogether pleased to see her; he had a wariness about him that made her hesitant.

"I'd like to talk to you," she said, standing by him.

"I can hear you," he replied, making no move to offer her a seat.

It hurt a little, as it was meant to do, but she was not that easily put off. Since he did not offer her one, she pulled a chair around from the next table, and sat facing him.

"Thank you for moving your things from the glass house," she said. "But it wasn't necessary."

"It wouldn't look right, us living there together," he said, and added, as if reluctant to use the word, "Unmarried."

"Yes, I know. I meant, I really hadn't planned to move out of the big house."

He looked her squarely in the eye for the first time since she had come in. "Maybe I was hoping you would," he said.

She sighed. She knew that the men in the room were trying to listen to her conversation with Jean, and she saw the woman at the bar, Liz, glowering at her. She dropped her voice a bit lower.

"That wouldn't solve anything anyway," she said. "I would still want Stornoway. Don't you understand, it's a matter of principle with me. I don't care for the house. I'll gladly give it away if you like—once I've gotten it."

"It's the getting it that worries me," he said. "I've seen what happens when people give all of themselves to getting, instead of just being. It's a disease, that starts the soul to rotting. This obsession of yours is a sickness. You got it from your mother."

"That's a terrible thing to say," she said.

"I'm sorry. I'm not condemning her, or you. But it's true. You start taking, and then taking by force and by wile, and after a time, taking becomes automatic, a way of life, and you can't even give any more."

"But the value of it doesn't mean anything to me," she cried, and at once lowered her voice again. "I don't want it for itself, only to set things right. Don't you see, I've been cheated. I didn't ask to be born, or to be born a Harrod. But I was, and Stornoway was given to me. It's rightfully mine, not because I will it that way, but by mere chance."

"It makes no difference," he said. "Chance may have started it, but you've followed through on your own. It doesn't make any difference if you put a cash value on what you're taking, either, that doesn't make you any less an opportunist."

She sat in silence for a moment, feeling dull and tired. She saw what he meant. One could be as greedy and grasping for a principle as for money.

"If you didn't really care about the money and that big house, you'd go away. Or you'd content yourself living there. You can't live there any more owning it than you can with Antoinette owning it."

He laughed a little at the quick change in her expression. "Yes, I can see you resisting that all right. You become a leech, clinging and clinging, trying to make the life there yours. But it isn't, you know. You may have been born in it, but you were raised differently. How is it you make a leech let go. Salt, isn't it?" He sprinkled some salt into his hand, and reached across, offering it to her.

She sat back in her chair. She could see what he

meant. She knew that in a sense he was right. But only in one sense. She could not give it up as easily as that. Her emotional investment in the problem was too great to simply throw it over. It had cost her mother her happiness throughout her life; she had never been able to be happy afterward, because she had remained haunted by her bitterness over Stornoway. And because she loved her mother, Margaree had never been able to enjoy complete happiness because of her mother's sadness.

"If I could only find the will," she said. She saw his face cloud with anger, and she leaned forward eagerly, grasping his hand when he would have pulled it away. "No, only find it," she said quickly. "I don't even care about showing it to anyone. I'll burn it if you like, if I can only find it, and prove it to myself, to you, to my mother's spirit."

"But why?" he demanded, not bothering to whisper. "I believe you. You know it exists. Your mother knew. Isn't that enough?"

"No," she said bluntly, "it isn't. Help me find it, that's all I ask."

"There's nothing I can do," he said sullenly. He banged the table edge with the side of his fist, angry that he had not been able to dissuade her from this foolishness.

"Yes, there is," she said. "You were there, in the house at the time. You can tell me who the servants were then."

"Why?" he asked.

The simple question excited her again. "That will

was witnessed," she said. "Someone witnessed my grandfather's signature before he showed it to my mother. He even commented on that to her. She couldn't remember afterward who had signed it, because she hadn't really paid any attention to that. But she thought it was two of the servants. And it would almost have had to be. I've thought that over before, and it couldn't have been one of the family. Think, who would he have asked to sign his will?"

He thought for a moment. "Old Angus, probably, the man had been with him for years, and they were fond of each other. But that won't help. Angus has been dead for ten, fifteen years."

She bit her lip. "There must be someone else."

"Mrs. Murdock, maybe, she was the housekeeper then. But she's been gone from the house even longer. For all I know, she's dead too." His face brightened as another idea came to him. "Hattie," he said. "In the kitchen. She's still there. She would know what happened to Mrs. Murdock, at least."

She was jubilant although she tried to remain calm. "That's something at least," she said. Even this faint scent of a trail thrilled her.

His eyes met hers across the table. Her very happiness at this clue saddened him still more.

"Give it up," he said, and added, "Please."

She did not waver in the harshness of his gaze. "I can't," she said simply.

He looked away. He looked angry again. He did not know what more he could say or do that would make her see what a dangerous course she was pursuing.

She got up. He would not look at her, not even when she asked, "Will you walk up with me?"

Finally, since everyone in the room was staring openly now, witnessing her embarrassment, she could only say, "Good night then," and leave by herself.

Her embarrassment revitalized her own anger. She thought he was the stubbornest, most unreasonable, most pigheaded man she had ever met, and she was glad that he had moved his things out of the glass house, not that she intended to live there, but this way she would not have to worry about seeing him again, or running into him accidentally. She hoped she never saw him.

But when she came in sight of the house, she thought how cold and unwelcoming the place seemed without him. She found herself wishing that he were with her.

CHAPTER 10

The conversation during dinner turned to the subject of Harrod Cove.

"Some sort of debris has washed up," Marc said. "I don't know yet just what it is. Something thrown overboard from a passing ship, I suppose. Some of the local fishermen have seen it on the beach, and thought they ought to mention it."

"Wanting us to get it cleaned up, in other words," Berthe said resentfully.

"We have an obligation to keep our public image spotless," Antoinette said. "I want the beach cleaned up."

That issue settled, Margaree asked, "Is there much of a beach for swimming?"

"A little," Marc replied. "It's rocky, and the water's cold. Why, were you thinking of using it?"

"I might." She had thought a sunny beach would

be a welcome retreat from Stornoway's dim and chill halls.

"There's a boat there," Marc said after a bit. "It's kept in a little metal storage shed down there, but the shed isn't locked."

Berthe, who had been listening to this exchange, decided that it did not interest her, and changed it to one that did.

"What are we going to do about a tutor?" she asked her mother in a whining voice. "Those kids are driving me crazy having them around all the time."

It seemed to Margaree that Berthe was hardly ever around her children, but she did not voice her opinion.

"I have considered several possibilities," Antoinette said. "I want to look into them a little more fully."

Berthe did not risk pursuing this further, and the conversation dwindled. Margaree could not help comparing it to the life she had known. Her mother had been an educated, intelligent woman, a woman of culture and taste, and despite the bitterness that had tainted her life, she had never stopped being interested in things. There had always been conversation, some of it bitter, but all of it intelligent, thoughtful, interesting. Margaree had abandoned the hope of real conversation with any of the Harrods. None of them seemed to care about anything beyond their own very narrow sphere of interest—Stornoway, some local gossip, their own immediate wants or whims. Although the house held pianos and phonographs, and books and paintings, none of the family seemed to have any interest in music or literature or art. The radios were seldom turned on, and there were no current newspapers or magazines. No one called on the telephone just for conversation. The people at Stornoway lived in their private world, encompassed for the most part by its walls.

Antoinette was intelligent, certainly, but her keen mind focused upon the narrowest of interests —Stornoway, her own comfort.

Had she always been like this? Margaree looked down the table at the older woman. Her mother had described Antoinette as gay and charming, not only beautiful, but quite captivating.

"She would charm the stripes off a zebra," she had said. "A male zebra, anyway."

Had all that charm and insouciance been a sham? Or had Antoinette changed so greatly in the ensuing years? Was this the result of living for a house, for a few material goals, without concern for the spiritual values?

The question she was really asking herself was, was Jean right in wanting her to abandon her fight for Stornoway? Perhaps he knew what lay before her because he had seen his mother start the same way, and had seen the results in her.

This question remained in her mind. She had coffee with the family in the drawing room, and afterward went up to her own room. But she was too restless to retire early. She decided that she would go back down to the library, and look among the books there for one to read.

Going down the stairs, she chanced to glance from a window, and saw that a light was on in the glass house. No one in the family except Jean ever used the cottage, and her heart leaped up at the thought that he had gotten over his temper, and had come back up, perhaps to move his things in again, perhaps even hoping to see her.

She did not mean to rest on foolish pride. She was more than willing to meet him halfway. If he would only make the effort to see her side of things, this entire foolish quarrel would be ended once and for all.

She went through the pantry, which was en route, down the stone-paved passage and around the great staircase, to the outer door. But outside the wind whistled coldly, and she went back to the hall wardrobe for a coat. She chose, without thinking of it, one of Antoinette's, a long, cape-like affair that came to her ankles, and that had a cowl, which she pulled up over her head to ward off the night's cold air.

The wind swept and swooped over the roofs, carrying the scent of stone dust and winter. The night seemed darker than usual. She walked toward the stableyards, pulling the cape close about her when the wind tried to whip it from her shoulders.

She had almost forgotten her accident on the stairs, and the fearful thoughts it had engendered.

But those fears had remained dormant in her mind, and now they crept out to confront her again. She was mildly surprised to find them still present, but they looked less foreign to her than they had before. There was a certain naturalness to fear in this place, that made it rather easy to be afraid.

She passed the canopied well and remembered the story Marc had told her of it. She had not felt the full truth of the story when she had heard it; now it came back to her with an uncomfortable sense of reality. A man had drowned here, perhaps had been murdered, thrown in to die a cold and choking death. In the past, perhaps no more than fifty or sixty years before, he had walked just as she was walking now, over these cold stones, perhaps dressed in a cloak like hers. Perhaps he had only strolled idly, or perhaps he had been oppressed by worrisome thoughts. While he walked, that well, which was his destiny, had waited for him, as it seemed to wait for her. She had a sudden fear of that pale stone looming before her in the darkness.

Perhaps that unfortunate man had heard the footsteps of his attacker, following him across the courtyard, moving slowly, but ever more swiftly . . .

She stopped, catching her breath. She had heard behind her the scraping of a shoe upon stone. Someone else was out here.

"Who's there?" she asked, turning around to look back the way she had come. The arches of the doorways were only dim shadows in the darkness.

The windows on this side of the house were all dark.

No one replied, no one stepped forward to identify himself. She was alone.

Or was she? The wind thrust down and lifted and swirled, and its sound was a great howling rush that might almost have been someone calling her name.

She shivered, suddenly colder than the night and her heavy coat warranted. She went on, but only for a few feet before she heard, or thought she heard, the sound of footsteps again.

Someone was following her. This was no casual stroll, else why would the footsteps stop when hers stopped? What need for stealth, where no evil was intended?

She stood in the dark shivering, listening, but no sound penetrated the sound of wind and a creaking shutter somewhere overhead.

She hurried on, telling herself that it was only her imagination that pursued her. She pretended to be unconcerned, but her footsteps went faster and faster, so that she was almost running when she crossed the last courtyard, toward the glass house.

Suddenly, something moved before her, into her path, a shadow darker than the other shadows, coming toward her; she gave a little frightened cry and froze in her tracks.

It was only a dog, a great shaggy beast who came toward her with a certain tentativeness in his manner, his tail wagging but his eyes wary. He wanted it plain that he was friendly, but he wanted to see too whether she was friend or foe.

She laughed a little nervously, and put out her hand. "Hello there, fellow," she said. He came toward her, sniffing. She recognized him as the big dog she had seen with Jean before, and thought that this confirmed Jean's presence in the glass house.

She was glad for the dog's presence. His tail swishing wildly to and fro, he trotted alongside her to the cottage, making the night seem less ominous.

Jean was not there, though. She stood in the open doorway and called his name, thinking that the darkened interior might mean he had already gone to bed. There was no reply. She found the switch that turned on the lights, and on an impulse, felt the brass openwork about one of the lamps. It was warm to the touch.

Her eyes had not played tricks on her then; the lights had been on before. Someone had been here, and had gone out while she was coming down and out. She thought of the footsteps she had heard, or thought she heard, in the courtyard. Someone going back into the main house? But why stealthily? And why not reply to her call?

Her new friend had come in with her. He sat in the middle of the room, meeting her gaze so steadily that she knew he wanted to tell her something. She decided after a moment what it was, and went into the kitchen. He followed her, tail thumping doorjambs and kitchen cabinets with a relentlessly eager rhythm.

There were a few canned things in the cupboards. The selection was limited. She decided that he did not look a vegetarian, and settled finally on canned tuna. She opened both of the cans she found, because he was a very large dog, and put the fish on the floor in a bowl. He sniffed, stepped sideways a bit to sniff it from yet another angle, and deciding finally that it would do nicely, began to devour it in greedy gulps.

She watched him eat, thinking that he was rather like Jean. He maintained his freedom, living as he pleased, and coming back here when he needed to. If he had found a meal elsewhere, she would not have met him in the courtyard, and she did not doubt that he had welcomed her as a last resort for an empty stomach.

It was not quite the same with her. She could see that in a sense Stornoway had been a last resort for her too. She could accept that it was not only an oath at a woman's deathbed that had brought her here. She had wanted all the things she had been deprived of, and her thirst for justice had been blended with the childhood dreams of her triumphant return to the castle. She had never quite shed the hope that she would find here something to take the place of the mother she had lost, of the family life she had been cheated of.

Before had been wretchedness and poverty and dependence; but perhaps after all it had been a mistake to exchange that for the present queerness. Because unlike the dog licking the bowl so that it scooted around the floor in a circle, or Jean, she had sacrificed her independence, her freedom of spirit. The worst of it was, she had gotten no more for it than they had, an occasional meal, and a brief relief from a cold night. And she was a servant, not to Antoinette, nor even to Stornoway, but to her own ambition.

She had no loving family, no comfort against loneliness or unhappiness. Here were people in retreat from the world. Somewhere in the dusty unused rooms of the old wing lived her uncle, a recluse, sometimes mad. But what of the times when he was sane? What did his world seem to him then? Antoinette had made for herself a duchy here, where she could rule supreme. And because she could not rule the entire world, she had no use for it. Marc and Berthe lived like little moons, reflecting their mother's pale light. And Ralph lived in a world of alcoholic fantasy as far removed from reality as Yves's world must be. The remnants of a great family, but no longer great, like the leftovers of a great banquet, shabby and unappealing, no matter how great the meal had been.

How different Jean was, a breath of fresh sea air in this musty place. No escape from life for him. He loved it too much for that, not as a Pollyanna, but on its own, real terms, and if they were harsh, he could be strong enough. What a man he was; a man one wanted to be woman to.

If only she could resolve this entire business of Stornoway, so that it ceased to stand between them. Then there would be nothing to hinder their love. She knew herself well enough. She might try to turn her back on this bitter legacy, and say aloud that he was right. But if she left this business unfinished, it would never quite leave her; it would always be there to nettle her.

No, she must see it through. Then, free of it, she would be his.

And because she knew that her love would continue through all this, she took it for granted that his would too. She was a little drunk on the newness of her love, and she would have thought it incredible that anyone could love less, or even differently.

"And I suppose now that you've had your fill, you're finished with me," she said aloud. The big shaggy dog had cleaned his dish and, concluding that there was to be nothing more, had gone to the door to indicate his readiness to be on his way.

She gave his head a pat, and let him out. He trotted across the courtyard, tossed her a parting glance over his shoulder, and was gone. She envied him a little his night filled with adventures, thrills, perhaps romance. The world was his magic kingdom, to explore, to smell and taste and examine, while foolish men slept to restore their strength for a day of back-breaking toil. And if he grew tired, there were a hundred sheltered spots in which to curl up for a nap; and when he woke, it was in joyful anticipation of the still upcoming adventures.

And she had a little room to look forward to, in a dark, eerie house, and lonely dreams of a man who might have been at her side, and was not.

She turned out the lights, and went out into the courtyard. She was a little sorry her friend had not stayed to escort her back to the house. But manners were not everything. Antoinette had them, and all in all, she thought she preferred the dog's company.

The fear of the dark came back, rushing down upon the wind like a living presence. She stood outside the cottage door, wishing there was not that long walk back to the main house, across two courtyards, past stables and sheds. She ought not to have been frightened here of all places. This was her ancestral home, and there was no one about but family, and family servants. The fact that she took no comfort from that realization deserved some notice.

She told herself she was being foolish, and gathering coat and courage about herself, started across the courtyard.

She had gone only a few feet before she knew that she was not alone.

CHAPTER 11

It was not a suspicion, but a certainty. She knew, with no real need of confirming evidence, that someone else was close at hand. She held her breath, and could almost feel the tension in their lungs as they—whoever was close—did the same.

She thought of the big dog. She did not know his name, nor if he would come if she called. She might whistle; but the wind was loud, and by now he was surely too far away even to hear it.

Something rattled, off to the right. It might have been a window or door shaken by the wind; but she thought not.

She did not care if she looked foolish. She lifted the long coat up and ran across the rough stones. The courtyard seemed to have grown in size, stretching itself out and out, so that it was an eternity before she reached the sheltering arch that marked the stables. She leaned against a column, breathing hard, and heard a footstep. She could not tell from which direction it came. The night, the echoes ringing from the walls about the courtyards, even her fear, confused her. Had the sound come from the main courtyard, which she still had to cross to reach the house? She listened, but it did not come again.

As a child, she had been afraid of the night. "Everyone is, a little," her mother had said, and encouraged her to overcome the fear.

She thought of that little girl, frightened, but comforted by the belief that once she had prayed, nothing in the night could harm her. Dark, dark, shadows dark . . . there was an old rhyme, but it eluded her, as insubstantial in her memory as the shadows moving in the wind.

The door to the stables stood open. She moved toward it, backing into the thicker darkness there. The scent of hay and animals that had once lived here seemed strangely comforting. The air was close, the silence heavy.

She had come here in the daylight; there was another door, opening directly onto the main courtyard. She tried to remember where it was. She thought there were stalls right along here, and if she followed them, they would take her across the building, directly to the other door.

She put out her hand, feeling—and brought it down on a man's arm.

For a moment the earth wrenched in its path

about the sun, and lurched. Her heart ceased its beating. A current of fear, like an electrical shock, shot through her.

Someone grabbed her wrist, so hard that even through her panic she felt the pain.

"Don't scream," a man's voice said.

It was a pointless command. Nothing, neither scream nor breath of life, could have passed through the tightness of her throat. She stood rock still, too frightened even to tremble. Something rattled in the darkness. Then a match flared.

"It *is* you," Ralph said.

The match went out. Relief came with the darkness. Here was no one to be afraid of, not even in the dark. But in the wake of the fear came anger.

"What are you doing following me about?" she demanded, jerking her hand free of his grip.

Another match flared. This time he was lighting a lantern. It flamed brightly until he adjusted the wick, and then settled to a dim glow.

"What are you doing wearing Antoinette's coat?" he asked, holding the lantern aloft to look at her.

She did not know if that was an answer to her question or not. "It was the first one I found," she said. "And you still haven't said why you were following . . ."

"My dear child, where on earth did you get the idea I was following you?" he asked. "I was here in the stables, minding my own business, when you came skulking in, feeling about . . ."

"What are you doing in the stables, at this hour, in the dark?"

"What are you doing skulking about at this hour, in the dark?" He cocked an eyebrow. But he saw that she was angry, and smiled. "Sometimes the women get it into their heads that I drink more than I should," he said.

She followed his glance and saw a bottle of cognac, half-empty, sitting atop one of the stalls. He reached for it then, took a long drink from it, and replaced the cork.

"I've finished my business," he said with a wink. "If you've finished yours, we ought to go in."

She nodded; she still did not feel calm. He put out the lantern, first opening the door wide to let a little more light in. Holding his brandy bottle by the neck, he escorted her out and across the courtyard.

"Wait," he said as they came near the well. He paused and, to her surprise, lifted the wood cover off easily. There was a little stone ledge running about its interior a foot or so down. He set the bottle on it.

"What do you think of my wine cellar?" he asked.

"I don't much like that well."

"Not like our well? Oh, I see, because of those stories. I don't think it's haunted, though." He put the cover on it again and gave it a thump. "Hello down there," he called. "Wait, don't move away, I'm only teasing you. Are you really afraid?"

"I don't know," she said.

He laughed softly, more to himself than to her. "There is so much, and so much, that you don't know, *ma belle* Margaree." He was thoughtfully silent for a moment. The edges and the underside of the canopy were wet with drops of moisture. The nearest of the stone nymphs glistened dimly in the dark. She put a hand on it because she felt oddly unsteady; it was cold and wet and rough to the touch.

He said, "You mustn't hate Antoinette. It's so foolish. A waste."

It was a startling remark. She had skirted all about that idea of hating Antoinette, but she had never looked at it straight on to see if it were true. She did now, but hate did not after all seem the right word. She was vaguely disappointed. She somehow had a feeling that things would be a great deal easier if she could hate Antoinette, and she tried to borrow a little from the man with her.

"Don't you hate her?" she asked.

"I can't see that that would make any difference," he said. "Unless you were trying to imitate me, which seems even more foolish. And what of the others, who care for her? Marc and Berthe think she's a goddess—not a very gentle one, true, but a goddess nonetheless. Your uncle, Yves, went mad with his obsession for her. A great many people think highly of her. It would be convenient for us if we could think of her as a monster, but she's really all too human. Driven, true, perhaps a little less sensitive to feelings than others, a little blind to life's beauties. She doesn't see things the way others do. Least of all, herself. I don't think she'd believe the way other people do see her. How do you see her, by the way?"

"I—I'm not sure," she said evasively. It was partly true, and anyway, she did not feel safe discussing Antoinette with this not quite rational man.

He chuckled, and they started across the courtyard again. "She certainly wouldn't agree with that," he said. "She's never uncertain about anything. It's a hard quality to live with, but an easy one to admire."

He paused and then, going back to his original theme, said, "It's a shock for anyone though, that single glimpse through another's eyes. Like a snapshot of a prison taken from a meadow outside —only, it's really from the window of another prison. Do you know Regnier's epitaph he wrote for himself:

> *J'ai vécu sans nul pensement,*
> *Me laissant aller doucement*
> *A la bonne loi naturelle;*
> *Et je m'étonne fort pourquoi*
> *La mort osa songer à moi,*
> *Que ne songeai jamais à elle.*

Antoinette is rather like that."

"But that is no prison," she said. "It *is* a meadow, pleasant and carefree."

"But you don't see that a meadow can be a prison," he said. "The vice of virtue, the virtue of vice, a mean contest, endless . . ."

They had reached the house. He opened the door for her, but absent-mindedly. She thought he had been talking less to her than himself. It was hard to gauge how drunk he was, only that he was not sober.

They had come in by the smaller courtyard, through the great hall. Inside, he paused.

"You mustn't be afraid of death," he said. " '*Là est le bien que tout espirit désire; Là le repos où tout le monde aspire* . . .' 'Here, the rest for which everyone hopes.' Good night, my dear."

He left her, disappearing into the dark drawing room. She wondered if he had another bottle hidden somewhere in there, but she had no desire to follow him and see. He would escape from the world, until such a time as he achieved that rest that came with the grave. He had no reason to fear death, because he had ceased to live.

She went slowly along the hall. But she had gone only half its length when a door that had been partly closed opened, and Jean stepped out. He looked as surprised to see her as she was to see him.

"They told me you'd gone to bed," he said.

"I had." She suddenly felt the full weight of her tiredness.

"Has something happened? You look upset?" He glanced in the direction of the drawing room.

She shook her head. "It's nothing. I was frightened, and then I've been talking death with Ralph. That poor creature."

"I wish you'd come away from here with me," he said.

"Let's not argue that again," she said. It was a sort of madness, she supposed. When he was not around, she did nothing but pine for him and want to see him; and when she did see him, they were at complete cross purposes with each other, when all she really wanted was to have his arms about her.

"You think I'm a stupid fisherman," he said. "That I don't know what I'm asking of you. You forget I did live here. I had all the things you're pursuing so relentlessly, and I know they aren't worth what they'll end up costing you."

"Perhaps not for you," she said.

He saw then how tired she was, and accepted her moratorium on their quarrel. "All right, I'll let it go for now. What I came up for was to warn you to take care here."

"What do you mean?"

"Exactly that. Antoinette is a very strong-minded woman who holds firmly to what she considers hers. If she ever learns that you know of that will, and are searching for it, that you might even be on the trail of it, there's no telling what she might do." Then, in case she had not gotten the full implication, he said, "She'd stop at very little to prevent your taking Stornoway away from her."

She was frightened all over again, because this

was so natural an extension of her own thoughts. She wanted to fling herself into his arms and tell him so, and draw strength from him. But she knew what direction his strength would guide her in; and she knew that once she started yielding to her cowardly impulses, she would never again have the nerve to see this affair through. She must hold stubbornly to her convictions and her own slim courage.

"Thank you," she said.

He did take her in his arms then, briefly, and kissed her.

On the landing of the stairs, out of sight in the shadows, Antoinette listened until the kiss had ended and Jean had gone away. Then she stole noiselessly up the stairs. She wondered what possible clue the girl could have to the hiding place of that will.

If only the girl had fallen for Marc; everything would have been so much simpler. "If you would put your mind to it," she had scolded him earlier, "the way you do with those silly girls in town."

"I have tried," he said lightly. "She's in love with Jean."

"Surely you have the charm to cope with that. He's not exactly a polished lover."

"Some women like that rough type. In case you hadn't noticed, your other son is"—he hesitated—"a different type of man."

" 'More of' is the term for which you were

searching," she said sharply. "You don't take this seriously. If she finds that will, you'll be an instant pauper. You won't care much for that."

"You could solve the entire thing by introducing her to Father," he said, taking no apparent offense at her insults. He knew that she cared more for Jean, but he knew that Jean would never be more than the two birds in the bush, and he himself would always be here at hand.

"And having a great commotion here in the house. I dislike that, as you well know. I would rather an accident, perhaps in the water. People are always drowning about here. It seems a sensible way of dealing with it. Didn't she ask about the beach earlier?"

And that was when, a smile brightening his handsome face, Marc had thought of the boat.

He was not, she thought, reflecting upon his idea, a complete fool. He had to be driven to act, but he could be clever if the occasion demanded.

CHAPTER 12

In the morning, Margaree asked the maid, Louise, about Hattie who she understood worked in the kitchen. But Hattie, she learned, was very old, and did not work a full day any more.

"She comes up to prepare dinner," Louise said. "To supervise it, actually. Sometimes she comes in the early afternoon, and sometimes not until almost evening. It depends upon her arthritis."

But this disappointment was offset by the fact that Louise brought with her breakfast tray a note from Jean. It was hastily scrawled:

I have moved to the glass house, so I will be close if you need anything. He had signed it and then written, as a postscript: *If I'm not there, I'll be taking meals at the inn and you can reach me there.*

So he was not so angry that he didn't concern himself over her, and she was no longer afraid, because she knew he was close, and she felt confident that nothing bad could happen to her if he were looking out for her safety. She felt certain that he would get over his stubbornness regarding Stornoway. For the first time since she had begun this business, she had an idea it might all turn out as she wished.

She was surprised to realize that his handwriting was far smoother and polished than his appearance would lead one to expect. She had to remind herself that he had, as he had pointed out to her, grown up in this house, with wealth. He had had good schooling, probably a tutor of his own, and all of the elements that made up what one normally called good breeding.

She kept peeling back new layers of his personality, to discover strange and sometimes contradictory new facets. It was like finding an unexpected and subtle new flavor in what you thought was a familiar dish. Yet there was something, an honorable quality, that you felt ran solidly through all those different facets—like the Christmas candy, that you could break anywhere and still find the same pattern intact.

Because she was in a good humor it seemed as if the whole world felt it must reflect her happiness. The others were uncommonly cheerful at lunch. Berthe seemed far less sullen than usual. Ralph greeted her when she came in as if she were an old friend. Marc was even more charming than was the custom. Even Antoinette, usually so distant and cool, seemed to be in a good mood.

She learned soon enough the reason for Berthe's improved spirits. Antoinette had decided that it would be best for the children if they went away to school. She had already written to the attorney in Quebec who normally handled their business affairs, asking him to recommend schools in that general area, and make the necessary arrangements regarding admissions.

Margaree had mixed feelings regarding this move. She felt sorry that the children should be shuttled about so, and made to feel unwanted. Moreover, she would miss them, since of all the residents of Stornoway they were the most friendly toward her. But the fact was, it would no doubt be better for the children to go away than to remain. At school they would have companions their own age; they would be free to play, to make noise occasionally, to express themselves a little. They would get discipline, but a less oppressive form of discipline than what they were plainly accustomed to here.

Ralph brought her thoughts back from this subject. "Cousin Margaree thinks our well is haunted," he told the others. "She thinks there are spirits in it."

Margaree smiled a little, to acknowledge his little joke, and to show that she was not seriously concerned about haunted wells. She expected Antoinette to change the subject; in the past, Antoinette had shown a distaste for the subject of ghosts.

Tonight, however, Antoinette seemed to have good cheer enough for the subject of ghosts, even. "I'm afraid we have no ghosts here," she said, but without rancor. "Had there been any, Aunt Helene would certainly have found them."

"I remember," Margaree said, stretching her memory back to one of her mother's tales. "She was very timid."

Antoinette nodded and smiled. "Terrified of her own shadow. She had three locks on the door of her bedroom, and she used them all every night. If a stranger came near, she fled in panic. She was quite a sight whenever there was a party or a ball."

That remark fell oddly on the ear. Margaree had never imagined Stornoway, except in her childhood fantasies, as the site of a grand ball. But of course they must have had them. These rooms, that looked so somber to her, must have been crowded full with grand ladies and handsome men, dancing and flirting while candles flickered.

"Do you never have parties any more?" she asked.

"My husband isn't well," Antoinette said, her smile fading. "I'm afraid it would be a little awkward."

Margaree felt foolish again; she seemed ever to be saying the wrong thing. "Yes, of course," she murmured, flushing. "How stupid of me. I forgot

... I hope I'll be allowed to meet him one day. When he feels up to it."

Antoinette stared down the length of the table at her. "I've been thinking about that," she said. "I think he would like it."

"He knows I'm here, then?"

"Oh yes. He often mentions you."

Margaree was pleased by this news, and embarrassed that such a small thing should give her so much pleasure. She looked shyly away from Antoinette; when she glanced up, she saw that Marc too looked pleased for her sake, and her feelings regarding him softened a little. She had been thinking of him and his mother as her enemies; perhaps she was being unfair. Perhaps after all they did look upon her as family, and wish her happiness.

Another thought, for which she felt vaguely disloyal, crossed her mind and gave her pause. If her uncle were really clearheaded enough to remember her, and talk about her, perhaps he was also clearheaded enough to remember, to think back to that other time, and give her a clue to the presence of the lost will. If she could meet him, talk to him long enough to judge for herself how sound his mind was . . . She wondered if Antoinette really would arrange such a meeting. There had been a ring of sincerity in her voice when she spoke of it.

And if not, perhaps she could arrange such a meeting herself. She knew where her uncle lived in the house. She had not specifically been forbidden to visit him, as far as that went. She had only to get past that dragon of a maid who, apparently, guarded him. It would not be too difficult to manage.

"Were you planning on going down to the beach?" Marc asked her on their way out of the dining room.

"I suppose," she said. She actually had given it no further thought since their last conversation regarding it.

"There's a nice little view spot," he said, seeming eager to engage her in conversation. "If you don't mind rowing a little. Just follow the coast around to the north, but stay out a ways, to keep clear of the rocks. It's worth the effort."

"Thank you," she said, giving him her warmest smile. He really seemed so eager to please. Something about his manner toward her had changed, but she could not quite put her finger on it.

He laid a hand on her arm in what seemed a truly impulsive gesture. "You're a very sweet girl," he said. "Isn't it a shame that we had to meet as we did."

He looked so somber when he said this, that she felt she had to soften the mood by saying sweetly, "Better than not meeting at all."

He laughed, and the somber mood lifted, and things were as they had been.

"I suppose you're right," he said, and left her.

They had been lingering just inside the dining-room door. She followed him out. Ralph was just down the hall. He had a magazine, and was looking at a picture in it, but despite this fact he gave an impression of lingering for a purpose.

When she came by him, he paused and said, almost in a whisper, "I want to talk to you about something. No, not just now, later. I was mistaken about what I said last night. Ah, here's my dear wife. Excuse me, please, cousin."

He went on, leaving Margaree to wonder about his remarks; Berthe, who had come from the drawing room during their moment together, glowered down the hall at Margaree.

Going up the stairs, where the rail had been repaired, Margaree wondered which of Ralph's remarks of the night before he thought had been a mistake. He had told her she mustn't hate Antoinette: Did he feel differently about that this morning? He had already had a drink or two somewhere, so it was difficult to judge how clear his thinking might be.

She paused in her progress up the stairs. He had told her too that she mustn't be afraid of death. Did he now want to offer a different opinion on that subject?

It was no use wondering about it. He had not offered any suggestions for a meeting. Presumably when the time was right he would see her again and tell her whatever it was he thought she ought to know—if he even remembered. She smiled to herself. There was always that possibility too, that it was not him but his liquor talking. The next time she saw him he might have completely forgotten his cryptic remark.

A short time after lunch she went down to the kitchens, hoping that Hattie might have come up to start supervising dinner. She had not however.

Margaree came restlessly back up to the main floor. She decided after all that she would explore Harrod Cove. Time was moving slowly; she was impatient to talk to Hattie, and follow up that clue. Perhaps after all some rowing would be good for her; at least it would pass the time.

She picked a book from the library. There was nothing recent there, and she guessed that most of these volumes dated to her grandfather's period. But there was plenty of Dickens and Poe and Thackeray. She picked the former, because his books had cheer and humor, and she did not need anything gloomy to oppress her.

She met Antoinette as she was going out. "If you're going down to the beach," Antoinette said, seeming to divine Margaree's intentions, "you ought to take a hat. The water intensifies the glare of the sun."

Margaree was surprised by that show of thoughtfulness and still more when Antoinette, at the hall wardrobe, said, "Here, take this one of mine." She produced a wide-brimmed straw hat. The brim was floppy, and sagged about the face limply, so that it gave a great deal of shade to the eyes. A green ribbon trailed behind it.

"Thank you," Margaree said, and went out thinking that perhaps after all her entire judgment of this woman had been in error. Certainly she was friendlier and more considerate today than she had been in the past.

But maybe, Margaree thought, crossing the courtyard, it's because I'm more receptive to her friendliness than I was before.

She saw the old well and smiled. Somehow, knowing that it was Ralph's hiding place for his liquor robbed it of its former horror. She thought that any ghosts hiding there would have expressed their disapproval of having their dwelling place used in that manner.

She paused at the glass house to see if Jean was there. He was not, although his clothes were in evidence. She saw that his room was neater than it had been before.

While she was there one of the maids came in with her arms full of fresh linen. "If you be looking for Master Jean," she said, pronouncing it John, "he said he was going over to Prince Edward's Isle, about his crab pots, and I was to tell you if you asked."

Margaree thanked her, and left her to her cleaning chores. As she came outside, the great dog came bounding across the paving to greet her happily.

"I suppose you've come to tell me about your adventures, and lord it all over me?" she said, bending down to stroke the massive head.

His tail beat a frenzied tattoo on the stones. He smiled and assured her with his eyes that he had indeed had a time of it.

"I'm going down to the beach," she said, going to the steps that led down. "If that's not too mundane for you, maybe you'd like to join me."

He had to think about that for a second or two. But with a toss of his head, he followed her. His general manner indicated that he would give it a try, for her sake, but he could not promise that he would stay if the experience proved dull.

It was a steep and tiring descent. She could understand why the present inhabitants of Stornoway did not use the cove much, since with the exception of Jean they did not seem the type for physical exertion. The steps went part of the way, down a steep section of hillside. They joined a path, that led down a more gently sloping portion; and when the bluff grew steep again, the steps resumed. The stairs looked old, but they were in good repair and seemed quite solid. She was grateful for the rail that had been provided. The climb down to the beach was not for anyone who suffered from vertigo. Her companion seemed to have no such difficulty. He took the steps with the ease of practice.

It was even questionable whether or not the result of the descent was worth the effort. At the foot of the steps was a small cove. There was not what one could rightly call a beach. Black rocks, far too rough for walking in bare feet, led directly into the water. On a flat surface of rock, pressed hard against the side of the cliff, was a ramshackle-looking metal hut, nothing more than a makeshift storage shed actually. She wondered that it had held up in the storms that she knew sometimes hit here. But the cove was sheltered. There was very little breeze; it seemed to have trouble finding its way past the protective cliffs that rose up at either end of the cove. The sun had no such difficulty. It was warm, and the water was nearly motionless, lapping gently over the rocks with a soothing murmur. It would indeed be a nice place for bathing in private.

Except, she thought, dipping her fingers in the water, one would need the constitution of a polar bear. The water was icy cold, despite the warm sun gleaming upon its smooth surface.

Or, she amended, certain other animals. Her friend had trotted without hesitation into the icy water, and was sniffing at something on a protruding rock.

She decided to leave him to his explorations, in which he did not seem to need her assistance. Boating appeared preferable to bathing and she went toward the little storage shed that served as boathouse. One came down the steps and across the rock facing its back side. On the other side the doors opened almost directly into the water. A ramp and a complicated-looking arrangement of pulleys and ropes apparently served to take the boat in and out of the water.

At the present moment, though, the boat was

gone, and except for some tools and a stack of paint cans, the shed was empty. Someone had apparently already taken the boat out. Or perhaps, she thought, it had been stolen; but on reflection that seemed improbable. More likely someone else had had by coincidence the same idea as she, and had only gotten here first.

She looked around and saw a magazine atop the paint cans. She picked it up and saw that it was the same one Ralph had been reading earlier. That explained it then. He had been in the hall outside the dining room when Marc had mentioned the cove and the boat to her. Ralph, who must have overheard that conversation, and who wanted to talk to her about something, and thought this was a good place to meet her, had come down to wait for her.

She glanced at her watch. It had been almost two hours since lunchtime. The poor man must have gotten tired of waiting for her and decided to go rowing. She had an impression that he did not often go much longer than that without a drink. She smiled, thinking that maybe he had a supply of cognac hidden around one of the rocks in the water, like pirate treasure. Probably he would row into view in a few minutes, his nose a little red, not only from the sea air, and his eyes glowing a little too brightly.

The dog had tired of the water and, clambering up onto one of the big rocks, was lazily sunning himself. She decided to follow his example and, taking note of his wet hair, picked a rock of her own, rather than sharing his.

The rock was warm from the sun's caresses. The wind and water had sculptured it into a crude bench. She leaned back against the hard surface contentedly, and opened her book.

She thought of Jean. A day before, she might have worried having him so far away. But today she felt differently. That sense of impending danger had left her. She felt at peace with herself and with the world.

A fly came to buzz around her. She swatted at him lazily, and opened her book to read.

It was a delightful place, and a delightful afternoon. No one could have been afraid in such a place, at such a time.

The afternoon grew warm. The sun moved lazily across the sky. She thought once she heard someone calling faintly, from a distance, but she saw nothing, and when the call did not come again, she decided she had only imagined it.

She felt far removed from any concern.

CHAPTER 13

When Margaree looked at her watch again, she saw that it was growing late in the afternoon. The sun was no longer falling directly into the cove, and the rock on which she was sitting was growing cold again.

Seeing her stir, the dog got up and shook himself energetically, his wide eyes watching to see what she had in mind now.

She looked again in the direction of the boat shed, and then out toward the open sea. There was no sign of Ralph.

She gave a shrug and started up the steps with the dog at her side. The water did not look dangerous, and even under the influence of alcohol, Ralph surely was sufficiently familiar with the area to be in no danger. If he had gone out in the boat and not come back at once, it probably meant that he was sunning himself at some other spot, where his wife or mother-in-law would not be able to find and harass him. Perhaps he had rowed into the village; it could not be a very strenuous trip from here.

Or perhaps, she reminded herself, he was not out in the boat at all. The presence of a magazine did not constitute very firm evidence. She might have been mistaken in identifying it. Or perhaps he had come to the cove and, discovering as she had that the boat was gone, dropped the magazine and gone back without it.

All of these possibilities seemed at least as good as the possibility that anything untoward had happened. Yet despite her line of reasoning, she felt uneasy about Ralph's absence, and the absence of the boat.

She reached the top and started around the glass house. There was little point in stopping there again, since the impression she had gotten earlier was that Jean meant to be gone for the day. The dog, deciding apparently that the afternoon was over for Margaree, parted from her at the top of the steps and went in the opposite direction, trotting along briskly without so much as a backward glance at her.

She came into the courtyard, and was surprised to see Antoinette and Marc walking toward her. It gave her a start to see them. It was as if they were confirming her foreboding. They stopped at sight of her, watching her curiously as she came to them.

"Have you been down to the beach?" Antoinette asked, and Marc asked, "Did you go boating?"

She answered "Yes" to the first question and "No" to the second.

"The boat was out," she said. "I've been reading and sunning myself."

"Out? But who could have taken it out?" Marc asked.

"Ralph, I think," Margaree said.

"That drunken fool," Antoinette said, with such vehemence that she startled Margaree.

There was an awkward pause. Margaree had an impression that they had a great deal they wanted to say, but not in her presence.

"He's been out quite a while," she said lamely. "Do you suppose he's all right?"

Marc assumed an air of nonchalance that did not seem quite right. "Who knows? He may have decided the ocean was whiskey, and he was going to drink it up."

She did not find that very amusing, but she thought that they certainly knew Ralph better than she did, and since they did not seem concerned, there was not much that she could do.

"I hope you enjoyed our little beach," Antoinette said, and it was such a pointed effort to change the subject, that Margaree could do little more than say she had and, excusing herself, leave them. She looked back once and saw that they were engaged in earnest conversation. It looked, in fact, as if they were quarreling. A nagging feeling that something was amiss remained with her.

It was getting on toward evening. She felt sure that Hattie must be in the kitchen by this time; she went directly there when she came in.

"Yes, she's here," the regular cook assured her. "Hattie, this girl wants to see you."

Hattie had been in the pantry on some errand. She came back into the kitchen slowly with a guarded look on her face, as if she thought the reason for the summons could only be unpleasant. She was a dark, swarthy woman with a vast bosom and she walked with a shuffling gait as if it pained her to lift her feet.

"Ma'am?" she said, pausing in the doorway.

"I'm Margaree Harrod," she said. "Margaree Butler Harrod." She paused to see if this information had any particular effect. The guarded eyes revealed nothing.

"Waldo Harrod was my father," she said.

"Yes, ma'am, and Miss Julie was your mother. I remember."

Margaree felt a current of excitement go through her. Someone who would remember, without resenting. "Then you know the circumstances of my leaving, and why I've stayed away," she said.

"Partly," Hattie said. She was a servant of the house, of long tenure. She had learned in her years of service a sullen sort of loyalty that had nothing to do with her personal outlook on things. Margaree recognized this hesitancy for what it was. Antoinette was mistress of Stornoway, and it could do Hattie no good to act against her in any way. But somehow she must get past the wall of discretion that the cook had thrown up between them.

She would not do it, she realized, with several other servants listening. "Is there somewhere we can talk?" she asked.

Hattie seemed on the verge of arguing that they could talk where they were. But something changed her mind, and she turned back to the pantry. Margaree followed her. They went into another little room used for storage of canned things. The air was stale and dusty.

Hattie waited with arms folded across her giant bosom.

Margaree felt as if she were skating on thin ice. She knew the wrong approach would only stiffen the woman's resistance to her. If only she knew what the right approach was.

"When I was a baby," she began, "when the old Mr. Harrod was alive, there was talk of a change in his will."

The thick arms came down. "I don't know nothing about any wills," Hattie said firmly, and started toward the door again.

"Oh, please, wait," Margaree cried, seizing the woman's arm.

"I don't know about any wills. I'm just a cook here. I have to work for my living." This last was delivered in a pointed tone.

Margaree sighed and let go. She could see that the woman was determined to avoid getting herself into any trouble. "At least tell me then," Margaree said, coaxing, "there was a woman here at the time, a housekeeper. Do you know where I might find her?"

"Mrs. Murdock?"

"Yes. She and the old man were friendly, weren't they?"

"I don't know about that. She lives in Quebec now, with a daughter." This information did not seem to her to be dangerous. She might even have been glad to have the matter put on Mrs. Murdock's shoulders and off of hers.

"Do you know the address?" Margaree asked, hardly daring to hope.

"I have it at home." She hesitated for a moment; then, her features softening a little, she said, "I'll send it up with Louise tomorrow."

"Thank you," Margaree said, her face breaking into a relieved grin.

"You're welcome, I suppose. But I don't know nothing about any will." With that pronouncement, she went back to her kitchen.

She pointedly ignored Margaree when Margaree came through the kitchen on her way back to the upstairs. But Margaree did not mind. She had gotten what she came after, another clue to the trail she must follow. And she would follow it, even though it meant traveling to Quebec City. She had come this far already, she could surely go a little farther.

In seeking out Hattie and trying to wrest information from her, she had forgotten the mystery of Ralph's whereabouts. But as she came down a short time later for dinner, she remembered him again. Hopefully he would by this time be in the drawing room with the others, looking not too much the worse for whatever adventures.

He was not there, however, and from the moment she entered the room she knew he had not been heard from. The people in the room showed it in their faces and their manner.

"Ralph hasn't come back yet?" she asked, looking from Antoinette to Marc. Both of them looked despondent. Marc had a sullen attitude; he looked like a little boy who has been severely scolded for some misbehavior. Berthe was by the fire at the end of the room, her back toward them. When she glanced about, Margaree saw that she had been crying.

"He seems to have gone out in the boat and not come back," Antoinette said calmly. "We've sent some men out to look for him."

Her manner proclaimed loudly that she did not expect the news, when it came, to be good. At the end of the room, Berthe sniffed loudly.

"Oh, Berthe, I'm sure they'll find him safe and

sound somewhere," Margaree said, going toward her.

"Oh shut up," Berthe snapped, so violently that Margaree stopped in her tracks, quite astonished.

Antoinette said, in her authoritative way, "I think that we might go in to dinner now."

The atmosphere at dinner was peculiar to Margaree. Except for the fact that there was less conversation than usual, and that Ralph was not present, it might have been any other evening meal at Stornoway. The people about the table seemed strangely unconcerned. It was not that they did not look sad; they did indeed. But they were not worried. Each of them seemed already to have accepted the worst, and was waiting only to have his expectations confirmed.

In the course of the meal, Antoinette said, "My attorney called today from Quebec. He's made arrangements for the children to enter a school there, at once. I will arrange for one of the maids to take them there."

Berthe seemed quite disinterested in this news, although it concerned her offspring. She kept her eyes down on her plate, and made no reply.

An idea came to Margaree, and she said, "Why not let me take them? I have an errand I want to run in Quebec anyway, so it won't be an inconvenience."

Antoinette stared hard at her for a moment. She seemed to be trying to read Margaree's mind. But finally she said, "If you wish. Marc will make any travel arrangements. All I want is that they go as quickly as possible."

Margaree felt that or whatever reason of her own, Antoinette was rushing this business of getting the children away from Stornoway. She did not, however, offer any objections. It gave her the excuse she needed for her trip to Quebec to find Mrs. Murdock, and she would enjoy having the time with the children.

They were nearly finished with dinner when the butler came in and spoke in a whisper to Antoinette. They all knew that there was only one subject that would bring him here just now, and each of the others watched Antoinette's impassive face. Margaree glanced once at Berthe, and saw that she, for all that she had always seemed to despise her husband, appeared genuinely grief-stricken.

Antoinette did not try in any way to soften the blow. She looked directly down the table at Berthe and said simply, "Ralph has drowned."

CHAPTER 14

It remained rather vague in Margaree's mind just what had happened that caused Ralph's drowning. He had gone out in the boat, as far as anyone could say. But the boat had not yet been found, which indicated that it had sprung a leak and sunk. Ralph's body had washed upon some rocks not far from the cove. He was not a very good swimmer, and presumably he had been drinking.

Poor Ralph, Margaree thought, genuinely saddened by the event. Hidden beyond that veil of alcohol had been a very kindly soul. He had been intelligent and cultured, and she had thought rather fondly of him.

Neither Antoinette nor Marc seemed to grieve for him much. The servants showed the polite restraint that was to be expected at such a time, but Margaree did not think Ralph's going meant much to them. Only Berthe seemed to grieve genuinely. She grieved, in fact, with a fervor that quite surprised Margaree, who would have thought the woman not very fond of her husband. It only served to remind Margaree that one can never truly know what is in the heart of another.

The confirmation of Ralph's death necessitated putting off any journeys to Quebec, for her or for the children, since they certainly would have to stay for the funeral.

The death of their father had not seemed to be a great emotional shock for the children, although they looked subdued and quiet throughout the period that followed. They had not, Margaree knew, been very close to their parent. It was doubtful if he had ever taken more than a casual interest in them, and they could not be expected to suffer the sort of grief that would otherwise be the case.

The burial was held three days later. The local churchyard was dominated by the huge Harrod mausoleum, attesting to the years in which the Harrods had dominated the village.

Only a few were at the services. There was the family, all somber in black, and the servants. A handful of people came from the village, but Margaree had an impression that these came more out of curiosity than out of any sense of grief. Berthe alone cried, sobbing softly into her handkerchief while the final farewells were said, and rejecting all offers of sympathy. She was particularly violent in refusing sympathy from Margaree; it was almost as if she blamed Margaree for Ralph's death.

Finally, the casket was lowered into the ground. Margaree would have liked to see a flask of brandy sent on the long journey with him. She thought Ralph would have appreciated that, but she did not think the family would take kindly to the suggestion, and she did not offer it.

Antoinette wasted no time on mourning. Ralph was buried in the morning. In the afternoon, she summoned Margaree to the room she used for an office.

"I want to have the children settled in Quebec as quickly as possible," she said, getting right to the point. "Do you still wish to accompany them?"

"Yes," Margaree said. "There's something I want to take care of in Quebec."

Antoinette eyed her shrewdly. "If there's anything Marc or I could take care of for you . . . ? Or perhaps my attorneys? I have a most reliable firm there."

"Thank you, but it's personal," Margaree said, hoping the other woman would not pursue the subject.

She did not. She shrugged and said, "As you wish. Will tomorrow be convenient for you?"

Although she was surprised at the quickness of it, there was nothing to hinder Margaree's leaving at once, and she said, "That will do very well, thank you."

So she found herself a day later rushing across the mainland on a swift train, on her way to the city of Quebec. She had the children with her, all excited chatter and happy laughter over this new adventure. If they had any remorse at leaving Stornoway, it was not evident. In her purse she carried Mrs. Murdock's address on a slip of paper. Louise had brought it to her room that morning as if she were engaged in an act of espionage. And in a sense, Margaree thought, she was.

There was only one cloud on the bright horizon before her; Jean had been angry at her insistence in following up this clue that he had given her. He had plainly not wanted her to make the journey to Quebec.

"No good can come of this," he had warned her morosely. "Let sleeping dogs lie." They had parted on a cool note. She could only hope that in time he would get over his stubbornness. The answer of course lay in finding the will and resolving that question. Stornoway was a wall between them, and not until she had effectively removed it would they be able to have any real happiness together.

Yet while she told herself this over and over, and saw the logic of it, she could not help being unhappy. She wanted Jean to approve of what she was doing. She wanted not only his love but his respect. She wanted reassurance, from him most of all, that what she was doing was not only important because of some past vow, but because it was right. And that assurance he still refused to give her.

There were times she wished she had never heard of Stornoway. She could almost wish she had been the tutor she had pretended to be when she first came, and not a Harrod. She might have met Jean, they would have fallen in love and married, living in the glass house, and there would have been none of these complications.

She knew what he would say to that. They could do the same anyway. There was nothing to prevent their marrying and living in the glass house, nothing as far as he could see. The complications were of her making. That was how he saw it at least.

But they weren't. She hadn't asked for them; they had been given to her. All she wanted was to unravel the knots in the threads that held them all together.

And, she thought, arriving in Quebec, Mrs. Murdock represented one of the major knots.

Marc had made all of the arrangements for them, and for the first time in her life she saw what a difference wealth and a prestigious name could make, even in a simple matter such as arriving at a strange railroad station. There was none of the turmoil of the crowd, no lines to stand in, no struggling to retrieve baggage, or to find a taxi. A distinguished-looking gentleman met them before they had even gotten off the train.

"Miss Harrod?" he said, tipping his hat.

"Yes?"

"I'm Paul Valante. Mrs. Harrod's attorney. Mr.

Harrod asked me to meet you and see you settled comfortably," he said.

"How kind," Margaree murmured. She tried to look blasé about it, and holding a childish hand in each of hers, gladly let him take care of baggage and tipping and all of the details she had looked forward to with anxiety. She had only to keep hold of the children and follow him about, and in a remarkably short time they were speeding through the French Canadian city in his limousine.

"My instructions," Mr. Valentine explained as they weaved through traffic, "were to see the children delivered to their school, and you delivered to your hotel. Mr. Harrod reserved a suite for you at the Château Frontenac. I think you'll be comfortable there."

She wondered if he knew that she had never before had a suite of her own at a hotel; for that matter, she had never even stayed at a hotel. Did he know that she was the Harrods' "poor cousin"?

They went directly to the school where the children were to board. It was in a splendid old building, and the atmosphere was less oppressive than most such institutions. The plump little woman who greeted them and took charge of the children was quite pleasant. Anne and Louis were polite and restrained, but Margaree thought they looked rather more pleased than not.

"Now, children, say goodbye to your mother," the schoolmistress said when she had done with the formalities and had the children in hand.

Margaree was embarrassed for the children, and said, "I'm afraid I'm only their cousin. Their mother wasn't able to come with them."

The schoolmistress gave her a look, not seen by the children, that at once said what she thought of mothers who were so very busy, and Margaree felt again that the children were in good hands. From an inner courtyard she could hear the sounds of children playing, happy sounds. She had been right in her opinion that this would be better for them than to remain at Stornoway.

"You must be very good children, and good students," she told them, stooping to give each a hug. "And I promise I'll see you on holidays."

They seemed equally divided between being sorry to part from her, and eager to join the other children. Margaree left with Mr. Valante, satisfied that the children would be well cared for here.

The school was slightly outside of town. They drove now into the city, on their way to the hotel. Margaree thought that Mr. Valante's remark that she would enjoy the Château Frontenac was surely an understatement. Her girlhood had been filled with tales of Canada and the Maritime Provinces, and the hotel's name had figured in those stories again and again. Since its opening in 1893 it had hosted, she knew, more great personages than any other hotel in Canada. The leaders of the Allied forces had met here in 1943, at the Quebec Conference, to map that strategy that had led ultimately to victory in Europe. The Château was more than a hotel, it was an historic monument, and she could hardly believe that she was going to be a guest in it. She thought, with a melancholy pang, how thrilled her mother would have been.

The car passed through a fortified gate as they came into the Upper City. "Quebec is one of the last of the walled cities in North America," her companion explained.

The street ended in a tree-filled square, the Place d'Armes, framed with colorful horse-drawn *calèches*. From here she got her first glimpse of the Château, its red brick and green roofs silhouetted against the brilliant blue of the sky. The countless turrets and spires towered overhead were on too vast a scale to encompass from so short a distance.

The driveway passed through an archway into a small courtyard. It was medieval looking and reminded her inevitably of the courtyards at Stornoway, except that those were usually empty of people, and here far too many people, cars, and bags competed noisily for far too little space.

Steps led them to the main lobby. Mr. Valante took care of the registration and the handling of her bags, while Margaree stood regarding the room and its inhabitants with a blending of awe and chagrin. She still had no really good clothes, and the cheap skirt and sweater she wore were rumpled from the long train ride, so that she felt shabby and out of place. The lobby was splendid. The painted beamed ceilings, the light filtering through the leaded windows onto lush Oriental carpets, the subdued manner of the attendants, all created an atmosphere of wealth and taste. All about her were women in expensive haute-couture creations, and it did not even occur to her that most of those women were busy envying her her pristine loveliness. She felt very much a commoner, and despite the thrill of being in this famous place, she was rather glad when they had arrived at her suite and she was removed from the staring eyes she had felt upon her in the lobby.

"If there's anything more you need, Miss Harrod," Mr. Valante said, giving her a courteous little bow, "you have only to call on me. Mr. Harrod said I was to do everything possible to make your trip a pleasant one."

She thanked him and saw him out. It was sweet of Marc to have made such a to-do over her. She was too inclined to dismiss him as a flippant young man, when it seemed that he was really very kindly by nature. She had known affection from too few sources in her life, and something within her responded far too eagerly to any act of kindness. The thought of the interest Marc had taken in her trip gave her a warm glow.

She did not stay long in the room. It was already growing late, and her return ticket was for the following day. She had not expected to need much time for her errand, and she had thought too, by keeping the trip brief, to allay any suspicions that might arise as to its purpose. She had gambled on finding Mrs. Murdock at home, and not away on a vacation or something of that sort, but she could hardly have engaged in an exchange of correspondence, even if the time had been available to her. She would trust in luck this once.

CHAPTER 15

It was nearing sunset when she came out of the Château Frontenac. The sky behind the hotel was red, and the Lower City was already in semidarkness. She showed the address that she carried to a taxi driver.

"This is on the Île d'Orléans," he said. "It's a long ride."

"I'll bet it's a longer walk," she said. They both laughed, and she got into the back seat. She did not mind the expense of the ride. She was enjoying the sensation of money to throw away on occasional extravagances, and when the driver, sensing some extra money to be made, asked if she would like to see a bit of the city along the way, she agreed without hesitation.

As they were pulling away from the Chateau, she sat forward suddenly, and nearly told the driver to stop. She had thought for a moment that she had seen Marc Harrod in the doorway of the hotel. But the taxi turned, and when she looked back, there was a fat woman in a print dress in the doorway.

Surely, she decided, sitting back again in the seat, she had been mistaken. Marc was at home, at Stornoway. There was no reason for him to be here; and certainly had he been coming to Quebec City, he would have told her so, and she and the children could have come down with him, instead of on the train.

It had looked like him in that doorway. But the very idea was so unlikely that she dismissed it completely from her mind.

They drove down narrow streets into the lower town. She saw a number of seventeenth- and eighteenth-century houses, some of them in the process of being restored. In the Place Royale she saw Notre Dame des Victoires, which the driver reminded her was the oldest standing church in North America. She could not help remembering too that Voltaire, with rare lack of historical perspective, described the Saint Lawrence Valley as "a few acres of snow."

The Île d'Orléans was reached by crossing over the north channel of the Saint Lawrence on a new highway bridge. They passed Montmorency Falls, which the driver informed her "are a hundred feet higher than Niagara."

They looked quite unspectacular to her, though.

The drive through Quebec City to get to the

bridge was the worst part of the trip. The road led across the Saint Charles River and along the Beaupré shore. This was once the largest seigneury in the country, but the venerable farms had vanished, to be replaced by a concentration of flashing neon signs, motels, souvenir shops, and scores of places selling those staples of the modern city, hot dog and *patates frites*.

On the island the road took them past small farming communities high above the river. From here she could gain a new appreciation of the Saint Lawrence, that widened to ocean-like proportions. On the other shore the mountains and clouds mingled in what Packman had aptly called "dim confusion."

A few miles along they came to the village of Sainte Famille with its lovely seventeenth-century church. The vestiges of yesterday were everywhere. The old homes had sloping roofs, and the thin ribbons of land were still defined by split rail fences. The whole feeling of the island was out of keeping with the present time.

The driver had to stop twice to ask directions. Finally he pulled off the pavement onto the soft dirt of an old, tree-shaded lane, that took them directly from the main highway to the seventeenth century. A quarter of a mile down the lane they came to an old farmhouse whose massive walls and steeply flaring roof must have borne the snows of nearly three hundred winters.

"Wait for me, please," she told him as she got

out. She gave him the money for the fare so far, plus a generous tip, and he assured her he would be there when she wanted to go back.

The windows looked dark, and she thought at first that her luck had failed her. But as she came closer to the old oak door she saw that the darkness was an illusion, because the lights inside were so dim.

Her knock was answered by a thin, waspish-looking woman. Margaree asked for Mrs. Murdock and, thinking it might help gain her entrance, added, "I'm Margaree Harrod, from Stornoway."

The woman who answered the door looked down her thin nose at her for a moment before partially closing the door in her face. Margaree waited patiently, and a few minutes later the woman was back to usher her inside.

It was an incredible experience, coming inside. She had suddenly stepped into a poor farm of 1680; almost nothing seemed to have changed from that time. The wide oak planks of the floor were bowed and warped. The windowpanes were imperfect, giving back distorted reflections of the room. The deep windowledges were cluttered with old bottles and a large crock, and plenty of cobwebs. The furniture was all very old, and gave off a warm glow in response to the fire blazing on the hearth.

Mrs. Murdock was a tiny sparrow of a woman seated at a table that was too small even for her. Margaree bumped her knees when she sat down at it, and she had to steady her chair on the uneven floor.

Mrs. Murdock peered intently at her through thick glasses. "My daughter said you were Margaree," she said. "Would that be Miss Julie's baby, Margaree?"

Margaree's hopes flared more brightly than the flames on the hearth. "Yes, I am. Do you remember me, then?"

"I remember, a little," Mrs. Murdock said. She sighed and leaned her elbows on the tabletop. "I remember Miss Julie. She was a pretty girl. And the baby, such a lovely child." Her eyes took on a dreamy, faraway look.

The waspish woman had come to stand behind her mother's chair. "My mother's memory isn't very good any more," she said, giving Margaree a look that warned her not to overstep the bounds of kindness. "She remembers Stornoway only dimly, and not very happily."

"Stornoway was a happy place, though," Mrs. Murdock said. "Before that other woman came and took over. Antoinette. There was an evil person if ever there was one. I was sorry to see her get the place when old Josh died."

It was the opening Margaree had been hoping for, and she had to seize upon it before the old woman's memory began to fade.

"That's why I've come," she said. "Before Josh Harrod died, he told my mother he had made another will, leaving Stornoway to her. But that will was never found, and my mother was disinherited."

"Yes, I remember the will," Mrs. Murdock said. "They never found it, though."

It was going better than Margaree had dared hope. "Then you saw the will?" she asked eagerly. Mrs. Murdock nodded.

"I saw it," she said.

Margaree took a deep breath, almost afraid to ask the next question. "Someone at Stornoway witnessed Mr. Harrod's signature on the will. Was that someone you, Mrs Murdock?"

Mrs. Murdock nodded again. Her eyes had taken on that faraway look once more, and Margaree knew that her thoughts were beginning to drift.

"I saw the will," she said." I witnessed the old man's signature. He told me what was in it, too. He said he was leaving Stornoway to the baby, Margaree."

They never found that will," Margaree said, speaking slowly and distinctly. "Mr. Harrod hid it. Do you know where he hid it?"

"Old Josh hid that will," Mrs. Murdock said, speaking more to herself than to Margaree, whose presence she seemed now to have forgotten. "Antoinette knew I knew about it, that's why she booted me out. But she never found the will. She looked and looked, but she never found it. It's still there, right where the old man hid it. Someday Miss Julie will come back and find it. It will serve that woman right. She was always evil. Evil."

To Margaree's disappointment Mrs. Murdock began suddenly to cry. She put her hands over her face, and her frail shoulders trembled with each gentle sob.

"There, there," her daughter said, patting her head. "It's all right, darling."

The flickering, soft light of the coal-oil lamps reflected off the old windows and sent uneven patterns upon the ancient walls and beams. The air was noisy with the crackling of the fire, the hiss of vapor from a kettle on the stove, the creaking of the old boards.

Mrs. Murdock's daughter looked coolly at Margaree. "I'm afraid you'll have to go now."

"But if I could only talk to her a little longer," Margaree pleaded. "I think she knows where that will is hidden, and it concerns my inheritance, you see. If she can just tell me that . . ."

The woman shook her head firmly. "I'm afraid it's no use. Once she gets to this point she gets all muddled, and ceases making any sense. Even if I let you stay and talk to her, it would only upset her more, and you would get nothing useful out of it."

She must have seen how great Margaree's disappointment was though, because when Margaree was at the door to go, she said, "Perhaps if you came back tomorrow, she would be clear in her head again, and you could ask her about the will."

Margaree thanked her, and went back to the taxi waiting outside. Despite the failure of this visit, her hopes had never been stronger. She felt certain that

Mrs. Murdock knew where the will was hidden, and there was a good chance she would tell her when she fully understood who she was and what the will meant to her.

They went back along the river, where the riverside villages were twinkling into existence, and through the garish neon jungle again. On the river itself riverboats, their gunwales awash under their cargoes of logs, and the seven-hundred-foot-long lake boats carrying the mineral wealth of Quebec, moved upriver toward the Great Lakes.

In a short while they were winding up through the narrow streets, through one of the fortified gates, and back to the Château.

It was too dark for Marc to read the dial on his watch, so he had no way to tell how long he waited by the old farmhouse. It seemed an eternity before the lights within had been extinguished, telling him the two women inside had gone to bed. He waited on, giving them time enough to fall asleep.

He had guessed her destination when Margaree's taxi, which he was following, crossed to the Île. Until then he had forgotten Mrs. Murdock. Somewhere in the past he had been told that she had come to her daughter here; he had forgotten it until now, and for that he was angry with himself.

Antoinette was right, as she usually was. Margaree's sudden visit to Quebec did have to do with that old will. There was no other logical reason why she should want to look up this old servant, whom she certainly could not remember from her babyhood.

Luckily, he had been near enough to hear that woman's remark to Margaree as she was leaving. So Mrs. Murdock had not yet told whatever it was she knew about the will. There was still time for him to see that she did not tell, ever.

At last he thought there had been time enough for sleep to occupy the house. He left his hiding place in the shade of an old oak tree, and moved stealthily across the grass to the back door. It had an old-fashioned lock, like many of the doors at Stornoway. He had plenty of experience with those. No more than a minute later, he had the door open, and was slipping into the darkness of that ancient interior. He had watched the lights at the windows. He was confident he knew which were the bedrooms, and he felt certain that the one whose lights had gone on and off first belonged to the old woman.

Mrs. Murdock lay in a restless limbo between sleep and waking. The storm that had raged a short while before in her heart had subsided to a sad calm. Her mind was crowded full with memories of Stornoway and a past that had long since ended for her.

She sighed deeply.

The door moved a little. Someone had come in. For a moment she thought her daughter had returned. What time is it? she wondered in confusion. Is it morning already? It seemed like she had hardly come to bed.

The footsteps, so soft you could hardly hear them if you didn't know to listen for them, came toward the bed. A shadow passed the faint glow from the curtained window, and she saw that it was a man.

She tried to spring up, and to scream. But she was too old to move fast, and the sound that came from her throat was a rasping groan of terror that was cut off as his hand slapped hard over her mouth. A light flashed into her eyes, blinding her before it moved aside. She blinked, trying to focus her eyes, and gradually he came into view through the glare.

"Hello, Mrs. Murdock," he said in a whisper, his lips very near her ear. "Remember me? It's Marc Harrod."

She remembered him. He was not much bigger than she remembered. Older, of course, but he had retained the slimness and handsomeness of youth. He had retained too that cruel look in his eyes that he had never troubled to hide from her, a mere servant. She remembered him all right. He had been a monstrous child, doubly so because he masked his cruelty and viciousness behind a cunning charm far too sophisticated for a young boy.

She glared back at him hard, trying to show she wasn't frightened of him. And she wasn't, just then; she was too angry to be really scared.

He seemed to sense this. Slowly, ready to put it back if he had to, he took his hand away from her mouth. He had cut her lip, and a trickle of blood ran down her chin.

"You," she said, her throat so dry she could hardly speak.

He seemed amused by her anger. "You know, you've made Antoinette unhappy," he said, "with all that talk this evening of wills."

She remembered everything clearly now; it came back in a flash. That girl who had come earlier. Margaree. By God, it was Margaree! And she had come about the will, old Josh Harrod's will.

As if she had been putting these thoughts into words, she said, "And I'll tell where it is, too."

"Oh, I don't think you will tell now," he said, his voice dripping with charm. He took hold of the edge of her pillow. "You've missed your chance."

"You shouldn't have come here," she said, getting her voice back. Her wits were coming back too. There was a big old kerosene lamp on the nightstand, just behind him. If she could get hold of it, and bring it down on the back of his head, she wouldn't have to be afraid of what he was going to do. She began to move one hand slowly across the bed, keeping her eyes glued to his to distract him.

"That's no way to welcome an old friend," he said. Her head bounced cruelly as he jerked the pillow from under her.

She tried again to cry out, but he didn't permit it. The pillow came down over her face. She tried to grab the lamp, but her fingers only brushed against its cold hard surface.

She thought, with a blending of defeat and triumph, "I always knew he had this in him."

He took plenty of time. Antoinette had long ago taught him the virtue of patience. Not until he was certain it was over did he take the pillow from her face and put it under her head again.

Then he stole from the house again, and hurried toward the place along the road where he had left the Rolls. It was still there, quite undisturbed. He got into it, and began to drive, quite slowly and calmly, back into the city of Quebec.

Back at his own hotel, he checked out, and less than two hours later he was on his way back to Stornoway. There was no need for him to stay on. He had accomplished what Antoinette had sent him to accomplish. No one would even know that he had followed Margaree into Quebec; from the length of time he had been gone, if anyone even noticed, they would assume he had been in one of the local villages, entertaining himself with one of his young ladies.

CHAPTER 16

It seemed to Margaree that her stay in the famous Château Frontenac was all too brief. She barely had time for breakfast the next morning before she had to check out and be on her way. Her train did not leave until afternoon, but she wanted time to look in on the Harrod children at their new school, and to pay another visit to Mrs. Murdock in her ancient farmhouse on the Île d'Orléans.

The children seemed to have settled in beautifully, with that quickness of adaptation that always confounds their elders. If anything, they looked a little impatient at her intrusion, and she stayed just long enough to wish them well, and promise to write.

It was still not quite lunchtime when her taxi pulled into the dirt lane that led to Mrs. Murdock's farmhouse. She hoped the residents would be up by this time, although she rather thought they were the early to bed, early to rise sort.

Mrs. Murdock's daughter answered the door. She did not look as if she had been summoned from bed; but she did not look happy to see Margaree either.

"It's you again," she said. She held a twisted handkerchief in one hand, and Margaree saw that she had been crying.

"I—I do hope I'm not intruding," Margaree said, torn between the urgency of her desire to see Mrs. Murdock, and her respect for this woman's privacy.

The woman gave a violent shake of her head. "Not any more you're not," she said.

Since she had made no move to let Margaree come in, Margaree said, "Will it be possible for me to talk to your mother again this morning?"

"Not this morning, and not ever," the woman said. Her voice broke, and she began to cry again. "She died during the night."

Margaree's hand went to her throat. She was stunned by the unexpected announcement. "Oh, I'm sorry," was all she could think to say.

The woman's grief gave way to anger. "It's your visit that did it," she said. "Getting her all excited, remembering Stornoway again. It was too much for her heart. It just gave out on her."

"I'm sorry," Margaree said again, inadequately.

"Are you?" the woman demanded shrilly. "Are

you?" She began to sob again, more loudly than before, and she slammed the door shut violently.

Margaree stood for a moment in helpless defeat. She felt agonizingly guilty over Mrs. Murdock's death. It seemed incredible that her visit had generated that much excitement in the old woman and yet, she was dead from it.

With a heavy heart, Margaree went back to her cab and instructed the driver to take her to the train station. There was nothing more she could do here. She felt certain Mrs. Murdock's daughter would not welcome her sympathy; and the knowledge of the hiding place of the missing will had gone with Mrs. Murdock, as it had gone before with Josh Harrod.

Antoinette was furious. Ordinarily calm under any circumstances, she was like an angry jungle cat now, pacing to and fro in the confines of her room. Marc stood meekly inside the door, watching her uneasily.

"You blasted fool," Antoinette said, sounding more like the wife of a village fisherman than the mistress of the elegant Stornoway.

"Couldn't you have asked her?" she snapped, stopping her pacing, and whirling about to confront her son. "All you had to do was ask her where the will was hidden. Then we could have found it, and destroyed it, and this would all have been ended forever."

"I was afraid she might start screaming if I let her talk," Marc said.

"Afraid." She made an oath of the single word. "Afraid that she would call out and bring her daughter running. Her daughter is sixty years old if she's a day. But you were afraid of her."

She began to pace again. She was struggling to bring her temper under control. It was useless to rant and rave like this. He had botched it, and that was all there was to it. She should have gone herself.

"The secret of the will's hiding place went with her," he said, managing a wan smile. It was difficult to pretend nonchalance in the face of his mother's anger.

"I hope so," she said quietly, bitterly. "I hope so."

Margaree arrived back at Stornoway in a dark mood, to find the household bustling with activity. She had scarcely gotten to her little room, at the moment quite a welcome sight, when Louise told her what the commotion was about.

"It's the annual Highland celebration at Ingonish," she said. "It lasts for days, and everyone goes. It's wonderful fun."

"Will the family be going?" Margaree asked.

"They usually do, for the opening day," Louise said. "But I don't know about this year, what with Mr. Ralph's accident."

Antoinette answered that question over dinner. "We'll be expected to make an appearance, of course," she said. "Berthe won't be going, but I'm afraid the rest of us will have to go. And of course all of the servants expect the holiday."

Margaree did not say so, but she looked forward to the festival in the hope that it might brighten her spirits. She could not share her unhappy story regarding Mrs. Murdock with the family, and it weighed heavily upon her. She could have told Jean, but there was no sign of him in the glass house. She supposed he was still angry with her for going to Quebec at all. Perhaps after all she should have listened to him; if she had, that old woman might still be alive.

That gloomy thought only made her the more depressed. She woke to a day that seemed as gloomy and gray as she felt.

Marc explained that there was a storm, a nor'easter, moving in across the Atlantic, and that storm warnings had been posted along some portions of the Eastern seaboard.

"What about the festival?" she asked.

"Oh, it'll go on," he said. "All of our servants except Louise have already set out. They'll hope it doesn't hit at all, or if it does, it hits far enough south that it isn't a problem here. A little rain won't hurt anything."

Shortly after breakfast, Marc brought the Rolls-Royce around to the entrance ramp. Thinking about the prospect of rain, Margaree had gone back to her room to change into warmer clothes. Louise, who would not be going until the other servants returned, wished her a happy day.

Despite her gloomy spirits, it did look as if it would prove to be a happy day. Marc seemed preoccupied, and Antoinette was if anything a little cooler than usual, so the drive over to Ingonish was a quiet affair. But once there, it would have been difficult not to get caught up in the spirit of the celebration.

As festivals went, this one was on rather a small scale. But what it lacked in size and pomp, it more than made up for in spirit. The entire town was in a party mood, and festival was everywhere. The local clansmen had donned their kilts, and the air was noisy with the piping and singing, and dancing in the streets.

Antoinette, who the year before had made a slight contribution to the construction of a new city hall, had been invited to inspect the work that had been done. She was met by the mayor, who took her off with him. Marc went his own way, advising Margaree that Antoinette did not plan on staying longer than an hour or so.

"Of course," he added, "if you want to stay longer, you can come back with the servants. They'll be staying until late tonight, most likely."

"I'll see," she said, and left him to stroll among the booths that had been set up along the town's main street. She hoped for a sight of Jean, and a short time later she saw him down the street. He saw her too, and came quickly toward her as if he had been looking for her as well.

She thought again, as she watched him come toward her, how handsome he was, and the mood of depression that had hovered about her vanished in the face of her love for him. She gave him a happy smile as he seized her hands in his and, ignoring the looks of passers-by, kissed her.

"You're back, then," he said. He studied her face. She knew that he was looking for news of what she had learned, or not learned, in Quebec. She did not want to discuss that here, in the middle of the street.

"Let's go for a ride," she suggested.

Some carnival rides had been set up in one area. They went toward them, and Jean bought tickets for them to ride a Ferris wheel. They got into the little hanging seat and, with it rocking gently to and fro, rose upward above the village. They paused at the top, with a spectacular view laid out before them, while some other passengers got on below. Then they were swooping downward, Margaree's stomach suddenly becoming tremulous.

"Did you see Mrs. Murdock?" he asked after another climb and another descent.

"Yes," she said, biting her lip. Her buoyant spirits had fallen again at the memory of that visit, but she could not avoid telling him about it. Still, she hesitated, trying to find the right words.

"Did she remember the will?" he asked. He had

seen that she was reluctant to discuss this, and wanted to know why.

"She remembered it," Margaree said. "She remembered where it was hidden. But"—she heard his sharp intake of breath, and put her hand on his—"she didn't tell me where it was."

She had to tell him the rest of it and, partly because she was honest and partly because she felt the need to flog herself, she did not spare her emotions at all. If anything, she made her role worse than it had been, exaggerating the excitement of that brief meeting.

"And now she's dead," he said, an angry fire in his eyes when she had finished. She nodded her head, miserable with guilt.

"And it's your fault," he said. "You killed her as sure as if you had strangled her with your bare hands."

It was one thing to feel guilt for something one had done, but quite another to have someone else accuse you of it. Because his accusation was too close to her own thoughts on the subject, it grated against the grain of her self-guilt. She was suddenly angry with him. He became the target for the anger she had been feeling toward herself.

"What a hateful thing to say," she snapped, her own eyes blazing.

"It's true," he said. "If you'd done as I said, and forgotten this whole thing, she would be alive now and you wouldn't be trudging about with guilt written all over your face."

She had been carrying the burden of this same suspicion with her since leaving Mrs. Murdock's farmhouse with the knowledge of the old woman's death. It was not pleasant to hear herself accused of another's death; it was far worse when she could not quite help accusing herself.

"And don't you have any guilt," she demanded angrily. "Guilt for the way your family has cheated me? You blame me for causing Mrs. Murdock's death. Well, I blame your mother for causing my mother's death, and it was a far worse death, creeping up on her over the years, years in which she had nothing but bitter memories. If you're going to go on about guilt, why not do something about that? Why don't you avenge me? If you think I'm doing things all wrong, you get Stornoway back for me."

"Stornoway!" He spat the word out as if it were something vile to taste that he had found unexpectedly in his mouth. "Millions of people have lived their lives in perfect happiness without Stornoway. What makes you think that it's in some way necessary to your happiness?"

"It is necessary," she said. They were almost shouting, and as the Ferris wheel brought them down near the street, two women passing by turned to look at them curiously. "And you ought to know why by now."

He lowered his voice. They were making their final round now, coming more slowly back to earth as their ride came to an end.

"And what about me?" he asked, his eyes searching her face. "Don't I matter?"

She was too angry to answer sensibly. The Ferris wheel had stopped, and as she jumped from the seat, she said, without thinking, "Nothing matters to me but Stornoway." She flounced down the steps of the little boarding platform, and went off along the street without looking back, her heels clicking angrily on the pavement.

He did not try to follow her. He stood looking after her for a moment. Then, thrusting his hands deep into his pockets, and muttering angrily under his breath, he went off in the opposite direction.

The infectious spirit of the festival no longer touched her. She was gloomier than ever. She had gone only a short distance before she began to regret her foolish words, spoken in anger. She paused once, looking back the way she had come in the hope that he would be following her. He was not, though, and pride prevented her from going to look for him.

She found Marc instead. He was engaged in a conversation with a pretty little girl with long dark hair. His flashing eyes encouraged the young girl's flirtatious response.

He saw Margaree and hailed her. He said a few more words to the girl, who giggled nervously; then he left her and came to join Margaree.

"I'm meeting Antoinette for lunch," he said, falling into step beside her. "Would you care to join us?"

"All right," she said without enthusiasm.

He saw that something was wrong with her, and gave her a quick, searching look. But he had enough knowledge of women to know that this was not the time to ply her with questions, and he let it ride, walking along with her in silence.

They came to a small hotel with a sign outside that advertised simply *Restaurant*. "This is the best place in town," he said, taking her arm to guide her into the little hotel.

Antoinette was already at the table. She nodded to both of them in greeting. She, too, saw that Margaree was upset over something. The girl had been like a black cloud since she had returned from Quebec. Of course, Antoinette understood well enough the cause of that, although she could hardly say so. She knew Margaree was depressed over what had happened to Mrs. Murdock, and she supposed, correctly, that Margaree was suffering guilt feelings regarding that business. She felt that there might be a possibility of using Margaree's guilt to her advantage, and she turned this idea over in mind. It looked now as if Margaree and Jean had quarreled. That was the only explanation she could think of for the girl's absolutely morbid mood at the present. That too ought to be useful in some way, if the right opportunity presented itself.

Antoinette contemplated these matters as she ate, smiling to herself. She had long ago learned that the unhappy emotions other people experienced—sadness, anger, guilt, pity—all could be used against them. They left people vulnerable, and affected their judgment. Whenever she had had occasion to attack anyone, she had begun by doing something to make them unhappy. Then, when she had them off balance, she had set about doing whatever it was she wanted to do.

She ate an excellent luncheon of cold salmon and a crisp green salad, followed by a pudding, and as she ate, she thought how she might use Margaree's unhappiness to thwart her ambitions for Stornoway.

The sky outside had been growing darker and darker with each passing moment. Now it began to rain, large drops suddenly beginning to pelt the window glass with a dark enthusiasm. By the time they had finished eating, it was a genuine downpour outside.

Antoinette ordered tea, and sent Marc to find out what the news was of the storm moving across the Atlantic. He came back with a gloomy report.

"It's moving up our way, and coming in fast," he said. "They haven't decided to shut the festival down, but they're considering it."

"I think," Antoinette said, putting her napkin lightly to her lips, "that we had better leave for Stornoway. I suppose this means we shall have to make do without any servants. Tell Joseph to keep everyone here till the weather breaks, or the storm has come and gone, whichever it's to be."

The servants had come in the shooting brake. It

was windowless and open to the elements, so that it would be impossible for them to attempt the trip back to Stornoway in the present weather.

Margaree, too preoccupied with her quarrel with Jean to give much thought to the weather, could not help feeling a bit sorry for Louise. The maid had looked forward to the celebration with such enthusiasm and now she would be cheated of her opportunity to attend, unless the weather cleared soon.

On their way to the car, she paused at a souvenir booth to buy Louise a present. She chose a little doll dressed in a Highland costume with kilt and bagpipes. At least Louise would know that someone had sympathized with her plight.

She and Antoinette waited in the shelter of a dress-shop doorway while Marc brought the Rolls-Royce around and opened the door for them. Even so, they got quite wet getting in.

Already it had become difficult to navigate the country roads that took them back to Stornoway. The wipers could barely keep the windshield clear of the driving rain, and the road itself was like a river of muddy brown water that seemed to threaten to wash them away.

Antoinette sat staring hard through the windshield as if she might actually will the elements to let them pass unharmed. And as they neared Stornoway, the elements seemed to bend to her will. The rain slackened a bit. Marc's hands relaxed a little on the steering wheel, and Antoinette could return her attention to the subject of Margaree.

An idea had come to her. She had always known that one did not always need power over others so much as the aura of power. A bluff was as good as genuine authority, if one carried it off well.

They were nearing Stornoway when Antoinette finally said to Margaree, "I think the time has come for a little frank conversation between us, my dear."

Margaree turned in the front seat to look back at her. In the mirror, Antoinette saw Marc cast her a puzzled glance. She ignored him, and concentrated her attention on the girl.

"I've known since you came to Stornoway that you thought you were the rightful heir to the place," she said.

"Yes, I do think that," Margaree said. "I've never denied it."

"And I know too that since you came, you've been searching for something." Antoinette was pleased that she had succeeded in surprising Margaree as she had. She had caught the girl off guard. That was always an advantage.

They were coming up the entrance ramp at Stornoway. "I suppose you know what that something is," Margaree said guardedly.

Antoinette smiled in a mocking manner. "You're looking for that silly will your mother went on about, aren't you?"

"It wasn't just a figment of my mother's imagination," Margaree said quickly. "She saw it. It was real. Mrs. Murdock saw it too, she . . ." She caught herself, and her face turned crimson. Antoinette's eyebrows lifted.

"So, you've been to see our old housekeeper?" She asked, quite amused at having tricked Margaree into making that admission. "And how is Mrs. Murdock?"

Margaree bit her lip. She would not be taunted into pursuing that subject again just now.

Antoinette said, "You're wasting your time looking for that will."

The Rolls had come to a stop. They were in the courtyard, at Stornoway. But no one made a move to get out of the car. Marc sat in silence listening to this exchange between the two women.

"It exists," Margaree said stubbornly. "I know it does. And so do you."

"It did exist," Antoinette said. She was pleased by the bewildered look on Margaree's face. She paused for a moment before she added, "But I found it long ago. The will you've been searching for so diligently was burned to ashes ten or more years ago."

For a moment Margaree felt her hopes crumbling about her. Tears of disappointment welled up in her eyes. Had she been pursuing an illusion, then? Had she gone to such lengths, for nothing at all?

Her stubborn spirit helped her now. "I don't believe it," she cried, tossing her head. She met Antoinette's steely gaze, and suddenly she was convinced that Antoinette was lying. What she saw in Antoinette's eyes was not triumph, but hopeful anticipation. Some inner source of knowledge told her that this was only an attempt to throw her off the trail.

"Where was it hidden, then?" she asked suddenly.

Antoinette had not anticipated the question, and she found that it was now she who was caught off guard. "Why," she began, and hesitated.

The hesitation was her undoing. "It was hidden where you never found it, isn't that the answer?" Margaree asked more calmly. She did not wait for the answer, which she already knew. She got out of the car on her side and ran for the shelter of the house.

She wanted to be away from them both for a moment, to calm the turmoil seething within her. She went to the drawing room because it was the first shelter she came to. Louise had started the fires against the day's chill. Margaree went to stand by one of them.

Marc came in a moment later. She gave him an angry look, but he only contemplated her for a long moment before speaking.

"It'll do no good to fight Antoinette," he said. She said nothing and when he spoke again his voice had changed subtly.

"Not on your own, at least," he added.

She turned round to look at him. "What do you mean by that?"

"Just that. You're banging your head against a brick wall, jousting with Antoinette. You'll never get through her or over her. But there are ways around her."

"For instance?"

He came toward her. He put an arm about her waist and drew her toward him.

"Don't," she said, stiffening. The thought of Jean was an open wound in her heart that pained her at the thought of a man's embrace.

"Why not?" he asked, smiling. "You've been mooning around over my half brother. But he can't give you what you want."

Her eyes widened and she ceased struggling against him. "Stornoway?"

"You think I'm a fool to bow and scrape before my mother the way I do. You think it's weakness. But it isn't. It's good sense. I'm her favorite, haven't you noticed? She may complain and fuss and scold, but she refuses me nothing that I really set my heart to."

He ran a finger along her spine. The gesture made her shiver.

"And you would promise me Stornoway?" she asked.

He shrugged. "I guarantee nothing. There are no guarantees in life," he said. "But I can get out of her anything that she knows about a will. She would tell me the truth. And at the very least, I'll eventually have Stornoway anyhow. She's getting older. Eventually I'll inherit."

She studied him warily. "But if you'll own Stornoway anyway in time, why help me take it away?"

"Perhaps I'm tired of bowing and scraping," he said. "Perhaps I would like to prove that I am my own man—as much a man as Jean, surely."

She nearly told him he was a fool; he would never be half the man that Jean was. But she held her tongue and thought for a moment.

"We could be allies," he said in a lower voice, coaxing. "On your own you don't stand a chance. But with my help, Stornoway can be yours."

"If I became your lover," she said, seeing the spark of hope leap alive in his eyes, "you would marry me when the time came, wouldn't you?"

"Of course," he said. "Not right away, you understand. Not until we've tested the water with Antoinette, so to speak. It doesn't pay to antagonize her."

"Yes, I understand that," she said. She knew that he was lying. He wanted only to make love to her. The thought sickened her. Even if she were not in love with Jean, there was still the fact that she and Marc were cousins; but that seemed no obstacle in his eyes. She kept her disgust for him hidden, and tried to think how she could turn this lust in his eyes to her advantage, and make some use of it.

"You'll find me a very pleasant business partner," he said. He brought his face toward hers. She closed her eyes and let him kiss her.

The kiss filled her with revulsion. It was the same touching of lips that she had experienced with Jean. But what a world of difference was there. Jean's kiss had been a sweet blending of their two souls into one. This was an obscene ritual in which there was nothing of the soul. His mouth closed over hers and she felt the hot taste of him and the pressure of his kiss trying to make her lips open.

He let her go quite suddenly and stood back from her, watching her.

"Well?" he asked.

"Give me some time to think," she said, trying to look coquettish. She hid her revulsion behind a breathless smile.

"Come to my room tonight and give me our answer," he said.

"Tonight? I—I don't think I should," she said, dismayed. She did not want to put herself into a situation from which she could not escape; at the same time, she did not want to cheat herself of any assistance he might be able to give her.

"It could be the difference between having Stornoway, and not having Stornoway," he said.

The door opened behind her. "I want to discuss —oh, excuse me." Antoinette stood framed in the doorway.

"It's all right," Margaree said, grateful for the intrusion. "I was just going." She went past her aunt.

"I'll expect your answer tonight," Marc said. She left without making a reply.

Antoinette looked after her, then back to her son. "What are you up to?" she asked. She knew Marc well enough to know when he was plotting some sort of mischief.

"I'm encouraging someone to make a fool of herself," he said, going to the sideboard for a decanter of brandy. He poured himself a glass. He had already had an enormous quantity of ale and wine and brandy but he had a head like teak. Unlike that stupid Ralph who had brought death down upon his own head, he was never drunk. Nor did he ever miss a point or overlook a nuance. He got along with Antoinette because he was clever, and could tell at a glance which way the wind was blowing. He had seen every thought as it ran through Margaree's mind—her attempt at flirtation, her hope that she could play him for the fool.

Antoinette did not push him for a further explanation. She knew at once that he was in a bad temper over something, and she knew from past experience that he would explain to her soon enough. She waited patiently because she was confident that his rage had to do with the girl who had just left him, and she thought that she would be able to use his feelings against Margaree.

Marc downed a healthy portion of the brandy he had poured. It was not enough to make him forget the recoil when he had touched her, or her resistance to his kiss. He was mortally affronted; he knew all of his faults, he thought. But a lack of appeal to the opposite sex was not one of them. There had been scores of young ladies all too eager to welcome his kiss. A hundred broken hearts up and down the coast could attest to his skill as a lover, and a hundred more willing to be broken by him.

He could bear insults enough. Antoinette often insulted him, and he shrugged the remarks off. But this was his Achilles heel, and no one had ever struck at it before. He was ready to inflict punishment on Margaree for doing so. Now he had to consider how best to do it.

"I've invited her to my room tonight," he said aloud.

"What makes you think she'll come?" Antoinette asked. "She's in love with Jean."

"She'll come. She thinks she can get me to help her get Stornoway away from you."

Antoinette laughed softly. "I don't care what you do with her," she said.

"She's a nuisance," he said. "I think I know how we can get rid of her. You've complained about her relationship with Jean. We can bring that crashing down about her head if we play our cards right, and humiliate her in the bargain. And if she's as much in love with him as you say, she'll leave Stornoway when I'm through with her."

He finished off his brandy. He would see that she

got what she deserved. That would teach her to shut her mouth and shiver when he held her in his arms.

Margaree went not to her own room but along the great hall and up the stairs at its end to the guardroom in the tower.

Back and forth, back and forth she walked. It was raining still and the wind had come up. She thought briefly of the storm moving over the ocean's surface, looming closer. Bad weather does not much help trouble; fine weather may make it worse. In a rich room one is isolated with them; a shabby room makes them seem worse. But an ancient empty room that has seen countless tragic events almost seems to cure them. One's troubles shrink when they come face to face with a collection of tragedy.

In this room a man fencing with his own son had stumbled as he lunged, and driven his sword through his son's throat. At one of the balconied windows on a bright spring morning a young woman had chatted with her friends until, of a sudden and for no reason ever discovered, she had stepped out and thrown herself over the balustrade. In a nearby room a woman had taken months to die, suffering horribly. Another had locked her door many times over every night, terrified of her own shadow. In yet another room nearby a young girl of seventeen had given herself to her bridegroom almost four times her age who had buried three wives, and lived to bury his fourth.

All of these unhappy people had had troubles and fears and sadness, greater than hers perhaps. They were dead with them. The curse that had driven that young woman to leap had fallen to the ground with her. The ghosts that had shadowed that old woman had ceased to roam when she had gone. That senile old bridegroom had gone at last to join his unhappy bride.

She was still alive with her problems, alive to deal with them and overcome them. If she took them to the grave with her, they would be with her through eternity, like these toys and bottles of wine buried in the tombs with the ancient Egyptians as company on that unending journey. But if she dealt with them now, she would be done with them.

Somewhere nearby lived a man whose tragic distortion of life made her almost welcome her human troubles. At this very moment he was moving about in a splendid empty honeycomb of rooms whose richness could no longer have meaning for him; perhaps it was better to be bad than mad.

She was calmer when she came down later. She went to the glass house to look for Jean, but there was no sign of him there. The rain had stopped momentarily, and the sky as she came across the courtyard had taken on a yellowish gray cast that was ominous.

She met Antoinette in the hall. "I'm afraid we

shall have to rough it a bit," Antoinette told her. "The storm is coming in fast toward the coast. The worst of it will hit south of here apparently, but the servants aren't going to be able to make it back before morning. I've told Armand to keep them over at Ingonish till the storm clears up tomorrow."

"Are we in danger here?" Margaree asked. She had never been through one of these nor'easters before.

"Not in the house. I wouldn't go out if I were you."

"What about the boats?" Margaree asked. She had thought suddenly of Jean.

"They'll be tied up. The people in the village have enough sense not to go out in a storm."

The sky grew darker while keeping its eerie yellow cast. The house was dark long before the hour for sundown. The lamps cast flickering shadows. The wind permeated the cracks in the old house and sent chill drafts blowing through the halls. The house seemed to wait tense and silent for the storm to strike. There was a crackling in the air that added to Margaree's nervousness.

Louise, on her own in the kitchen, had managed to put together a creditable dinner of cold beef and various side dishes. She hurried from kitchen to dining room, trying to be both places at once and looking flushed. Margaree thought Antoinette ought to thank her for her extra efforts, but the idea seemed not to occur to Antoinette.

Marc was attentive and more than usually

charming. Several times in handing her dishes he let his hand touch hers and in that simple gesture he was able to imply a great intimacy. She tried to flirt back and pretend to be flattered by his overtures. She had put off the final decision regarding his suggestion, but the time was approaching when it could be put off no longer.

He followed her from the dining room, moving close to her to ask in a whisper, "Will you come to my room, tonight?"

"Yes," she said, and went on.

She had made up her mind to try to make an ally of Marc. She knew that she must disappoint him in his romantic desires. It was useless to think that she could become his lover when she cared for no one but Jean. But she felt confident that she could make him accept this, and perhaps still enlist his aid in her plans. He had indicated that he was weary of Antoinette's domination and would enjoy a bit more freedom. Working together, he could achieve that goal while helping her to achieve hers.

So she could come to his room, not for the purpose he had in mind, but to discuss all this with him, to plead with him if need be. He was a bit immature, but he was intelligent nonetheless; if she could convince him of the benefits to him, her battle would be half won.

The shutters had been put up about the house. Fires were lit. In her own room, with the fire hissing and crackling on the hearth, and the windows sealed, she felt completely cut off from the outside world. She wished Jean were here, but she supposed he would be staying in the village until the storm was safely past. She stared into the flames and felt as if she were drawing not only light and warmth from them, but a source of power as well that might burn within her and help her in her meeting with Marc.

At last she felt that the time was right. She was wearing a simple blouse and skirt. She donned a sweater as well, not only for warmth, but because she wanted to be more than ordinarily clothed.

The house was ominously silent. There were no servants about, no sign of life at all in fact. The winds whipping through the halls sent the hanging lights dancing, so that the shadows seemed to leap about, sometimes beckoning her, sometimes mocking her. She felt as if she were walking through throngs of ghosts, each with its own timeless story to tell, if she would but pause and listen.

She knew well enough which room was Marc's. The door was closed; she knocked lightly, and he opened it almost at once. He was wearing a robe. Another time she might have modestly declined to come into his room, with him dressed as he was. But this was no time for such considerations as that, she reminded herself. She came in, and he closed the door after her.

The fire was burning here as well, casting its dancing shadows. His bed had been turned down. The chairs had been put close together before the fire, and on the table before them was a tray with liquors and glasses. It was a romantic enough setting. If she were another girl, or he another man, it might have been perfect.

He saw her glance at the table, and said, "Would you like a drink?"

"Thank you, no," she said. "I didn't come for that."

"But you came," he said. He was smiling, in a way that she found objectionable. His eyes caught the gleam of the fire and sent it warmed back to her. Her uneasiness was multiplying. He looked so very intent upon his romantic purpose; perhaps she had made a mistake in coming here, and trying to use this time and setting to convince him of her ideas.

"I did come, yes, but . . ." she tried to say, stammering a little.

"Stornoway means everything to you, doesn't it?" he interrupted her. He moved toward her.

She edged backward, but the chair was in her way. She bumped into it, and stood still.

"It means a great deal," she said, frightened by what she saw written boldly across his face. There was everything there but the friendship she thought she could play upon. She saw lust and greed and even hatred. She wished suddenly and fervently that she had not come. She glanced past him at the door.

He seized that moment to move, with the lightness of a cat, across the space between them. Before she knew what was happening, even, she was in his arms, and his mouth was upon hers.

For a moment she was frozen in bewildered helplessness. Then, as his kiss grew ardent and demanding, she tried to struggle against him. He was stronger than he looked, and he held her in a grip like iron. Her efforts to free herself became more violent. She pushed against his chest with the flat of her hands, but he held her fast.

As suddenly as he had seized her, he released her. She staggered sideways, caught off balance by the suddenness with which he had let her go. Her face was flushed with fear and anger.

But to the unknowing eye, those emotions looked much the same as passion. She heard a sound and looked toward the hall door. To her horror, she saw that it was open. Framed in the opening was Jean, and behind him his mother. Antoinette was smiling, a look of triumph lighting her handsome face.

Margaree's eyes met those of her beloved; that meeting of glances was like a physical blow. She saw not the love that she had come to look for in his eyes, but the opposite emotions—loathing, disgust, anger. He looked as if he could come to her and strike her; she almost wished that he would. Anything must surely be better than this cold fury with which he now regarded her.

"Jean," was all she could say. She saw at once that she had been tricked. Marc and Antoinette had set a trap for her, with this moment as its goal, and she had walked blindly, foolishly into it. But what could she say that would make him understand that, that would erase the picture that was before his eyes with all its false implications.

When he spoke, his every word and tone condemned her. His voice was like the lash of a whip over her.

"You would do anything at all, wouldn't you, to achieve your greedy ambitions?" he asked. "Even giving yourself to my brother?"

"Jean, please," she said, coming toward him with outstretched hands. "You don't understand."

He struck her hands away. "I understand enough," he cried. "Damn you!"

He suddenly whirled about and, nearly knocking his mother aside, ran down the hall.

Margaree ran into the hall after him. "Jean," she cried. But he ran on without slowing his pace. In a moment he had disappeared on the stairs.

She stood among the halls' dancing shadows, tears burning her eyes. Behind her, Marc and Antoinette laughed loud and derisively.

CHAPTER 17

Margaree ran from them, along the dim corridors, to the haven of her own room. She was appalled by what Jean had thought and of what he had accused her. Thank God he was wrong at least. He might be angry, but she was innocent of his charge, and she had confidence in the power of right to prevail.

She thought of his accusation—that she would give herself to Marc to gain Stornoway—as a stone flung at her in anger, that had luckily missed its mark. But when she passed Louise in the hall, she caught herself blushing for no reason at all, and she realized that the accusation was not a stone at all, but a net that had been flung over her, and from which she could not escape.

Louise saw the blush even in the dim light and

gave her a curious look. Margaree ran past her, to her room, and closed the door soundly.

It is a frightful experience to discover that misconceptions can carry any weight, and perhaps even have within them the germ of truth. Nothing gives more of a sense of helplessness than their not entirely unjust weight.

She sat down in front of the fire, feeling completely overwhelmed by her anguish. She felt penetrated by the ugly wickedness of the world. She hated all of life, even herself, because she was alive. She hated herself most of all, for having walked with open eyes into this sorry business. She ought never to have come to Stornoway. She ought to go away now.

One of the shutters at her window had come loose. Now quite suddenly the wind outside seized it and sent it crashing open, and the next moment the glass shattered into the room. She jumped at the sudden onslaught of sound and wind and rain. But it was the interruption that she needed in her train of thoughts. By the time she had struggled with the shutter and managed to get it fastened again, she was cold and drenched with rain; but she was also over the emotional shock of the scene she had just played a part in.

She stood shivering in front of the fire, and saw that it was no good upbraiding herself for what had gone before. It was no longer a question of whether she should have come to Stornoway or not. She had come, she was here. And thank God, she thought fervently. Because if she had not, she would not have met Jean, and never have known the wonder of the love she felt for him.

The sudden realization of her great love was like a dash of cold water. She loved him! Far more than Stornoway, far more important than any deathbed promise was he to her. She had been blinded by an obsession. He had been at least partly right, she had been driven by greed; not her own, necessarily, but greed nonetheless. She had become so determined to have Stornoway for her mother's sake that she had sacrificed her own principles, her life, her love for Jean. Perhaps he had seen things more clearly than she a few moments before; perhaps she would have gone so far as to give herself to Marc to obtain her goal.

She had been a fool. He had been right to try to persuade her to give up her ambition to own Stornoway. He had been right to be angry, and to rush out of her life. It was she who had been wrong. She had nearly committed a deep wrong against him, against herself, for the sake of nothing more endearing than a house, a house she didn't even much care for. For the sake of these cold, shadowy halls, she had refused happiness with him in the glass house.

"I've been asleep and dreaming," she said aloud, staring into the fire.

But now she was awake. Now she saw, when she had perhaps lost him, how much Jean meant to her. She would rather live with him in a cottage than be mistress of Stornoway without him. This was what mattered.

Had she lost him?

It mustn't be! She had to find him, now, at once, and tell him how wrong she had been. She would be his slave if he wished, if only he would forgive her, at once, so that she could forgive herself.

She ran from her room, along the hall again, and down the twisting stairs. She saw no one, and she was grateful. Had she had to face Marc or Antoinette now, in her present frame of mind, there was no telling what she might have done or said. They were evil, selfish, and blind to all goodness and beauty.

And she had tried to emulate them!

She took a slicker from the wardrobe in the hall, and ran from the house.

The storm was frightful. The wind tore through the arches, whipping her coat about her. It was like the hand of judgment pressing down upon her. She stood for a moment in the courtyard, swaying as she tried to get her balance against it. Then, moving slowly despite her efforts, she crossed the courtyards to the glass house.

Jean was not there. She stood indecisively within the cottage for a moment. The storm was getting worse with each passing minute. It was dangerous to try to go down to the village in that wind and rain.

But more dangerous, she thought, going back out, to stay here. Going out she could lose at the very worst her life. But by staying here she risked losing something far more precious to her than her life.

It was an arduous trip down to the village, struggling against the storm. The wind, rushing in from the sea, was against her, so that she had to lean against it, and several times she nearly fell. But the thought of Jean drove her on and gave her a strength she would never have dreamed she possessed. She did not think of herself as brave in doing this, but as desperate.

She went first to the wharf, not so much reasoning that she might find him there, as because it was the closest of the possible destinations. But there was no sign of his boat in the water. She stood for a moment watching the other boats toss about on the violent waves, sometimes crashing against one another, sometimes scraping the dock. Surely Jean was too good a sailor to risk staying out in this weather. He must have come straight here from the house and, in his anger, taken the boat out. But he would see how dangerous it was, and bring it back to the harbor.

After a moment, she decided that he might have taken the boat to some more sheltered spot. That was more logical. He loved his boat more than anything else. Even in anger he would not jeopardize it in a storm.

She left the wharf and went toward the inn. It was not very late yet, but the town gave the impression of a ghost town. The streets were dark.

The windows of the buildings she passed were shuttered. As she went past some of them she saw little fingers of light, and knew that for all the darkness and stillness, few people would be sleeping. The storm meant more to the people down here than it would to those who lived at Stornoway. Undoubtedly there must be some ships that had not come home, sailors who had stayed over in another town, and even some who right now were risking the perilous waves to reach the village. Behind some of these shutters families waited and prayed. For others the storm might mean damage to their ships in the harbor, and perhaps the loss of their livelihood.

The windows of the inn were shuttered as well, but she saw light from within, and over the roar of the storm she heard the tinkling of music. She pounded on the door and cried out to be let in, hardly able to hear her own shouting over the wind. But after a minute the door opened and she hurried in.

The room was bright with lights and blazing fires. Someone had set an old-fashioned looking phonograph up on the bar, and it was playing a record loudly. There were thirty, maybe forty men here, waiting out the storm and drinking in the meantime to ease their concern. They all turned as she came in and looked curiously at her. No one expected a woman to be out on this night; perhaps some irate wife, frightened at home alone and seeking out her husband to take him home with her; or

Liz, who was different. But not this woman from the big house, who by rights ought to be tucked safely within Stornoway's walls just now. She looked frail and frightened, and each of those coarse men felt the same urge to jump to her side and shelter her in his arms.

It was the widow, Liz, who had let her inside and who now shoved the thick oak door shut behind her, giving the curtains a rest from the wind that had billowed them. The tavern woman stood by the door, eying Margaree in a curious and not very friendly fashion.

"Is Jean Copley here?" Margaree asked. Her eyes had already searched the sea of faces turned toward her. Jean's face had not been among them; she felt as if she could cry with frustration, but she could not do so before all those curious stares.

The woman at the door shrugged. "See for yourself," she said, indicating the room.

Margaree's heart sank still lower. Before, struggling through the storm, she had been too concerned with getting here and finding Jean to think of how fatigued she was becoming. But the warmth and bustle of the room, the loud music and clinking glasses, the curious stares and her own sense of disappointment, combined to weigh upon her shoulders like a mantle of exhaustion. She would have liked to drop into one of those chairs and rest. But she could not, not until she had found Jean.

"Has he been in?" she asked. The answer was another shrug.

She felt defeated and weary. She tried to think, becoming increasingly aware of the many men watching her. He wasn't here. That could only mean he was on his boat—but where?

Perhaps he had after all taken the boat out in a fit of anger. If so, he might even now be struggling back to the harbor's shelter. She could think of nothing else to do but to return to the wharf.

"Tell him I came looking for him," she said to the plump woman at the door. She pulled the door open again. The wind rattled glasses on the bar and sent the flames in the fireplace leaping and swirling. Margaree went out, tugging the door shut after herself.

Liz brought the heavy bolt down across the door again, locking it not against any human intruder— every man was welcome here on a night like this— but against the wily gusts of wind that searched incessantly for an entrance to the room.

She thought the girl from the big house was a fool to be out on this night. She would break her neck. That thought made the widow smile. She hoped that that did happen. How she hated her, that pale, fragile-looking creature with her tiny waist and her great wide eyes. Before she had come, Jean had been sweet and loving with her, and she had been able to dream that someday she would have more than a few stealthy nights each month. But all of that had changed. Jean no longer joked or flirted with her, and he had not come stealing to her arms since that girl had arrived.

She hoped the storm carried her out to sea and drowned her!

She turned from the door, and saw that the camaraderie that had been burning strong among the men had faltered in the face of the intrusion. The men had masked their concern with an air of gaiety and a pint of ale. But how could they be gay when a frightened-looking girl was out in this weather?

"Well," Liz said, her pink face breaking into a big smile, "has everyone gone to sleep? Come on, boys, let's all have a drink, on the house."

The music had stopped. She went quickly to the phonograph and put on another record, turning the volume as high as it would go. It was a polka. It rang raucously from the speaker, effectively hiding the noise of the wind outside.

She turned to the first man along the bar, a tall bearded man in a tattered coat.

"Come on, Pete," she cried, seizing his arm, "let's show them how they do it in the Highlands."

He laughed and began to dance with her.

"That's not the way it goes," someone else shouted. Another man jumped up and grabbed Liz from Pete's embrace. She came laughing into his arms.

"Like this," the newcomer cried, and began to whirl about the room with his partner, banging into tables and chairs without slowing his pace. Liz threw her head back and laughed like a sailor. The music blared. Everyone forgot the pale girl who had come for a minute and gone again.

Hardly anyone noticed when Jean Copley came in from the back way. He was soaked through to the skin, because he hadn't been wearing a slicker. He had come down from Stornoway in a fury of anger. But the sight of his boat bobbing helplessly about in the harbor had distracted him from the scene he had just witnessed. His boat was in a vulnerable spot, between a big schooner and the dock itself, the one crashing it with every wave against the other. He knew of a sheltered cove where his little boat could ride out the storm safely. He was not afraid to take her out just now; he could sail the waves like old Neptune himself. The worst was yet to come, and he wanted the boat safe before that.

So he had taken her to the cove, scarcely more than a mile along the cliffs, and now he was back, and could forget about her until the storm was passed.

He came along the unlighted back hall, past the stairs that led to the widow's bedroom upstairs. The back door was never locked. He had come often enough in the night, to climb those stairs.

He went past them now though. He had lost all taste for the stairs and what they meant. He entered the noisy barroom and made his way through the crowds to the bar. The man who helped Liz with the serving was behind it just now. He brought Jean a stein of ale.

He sat staring down at the dirty floor with its carpet of sawdust and cigarette butts. A pair of buckled shoes came into view and above them slim ankles led his eye upward until he was looking into Liz's smiling face.

"Looks like it'll blow in here for sure," she said. She was standing close, so that he could smell the scent of her perfume and, less powerful, sweat from the polka she had been dancing.

"It's headed south," he said. "We'll get the tail of it is all." He made it sound deprecating. Both of them knew that the tail of a nor'easter was enough to flatten a house or swamp a good ship.

"Have you seen to your boat?" she asked. He nodded. "Then I suppose," she said, the corners of her mouth curling upward sharply, "you won't be going back out again this night?"

He knew what she was leading up to, and that thought made her smile. But he hadn't the stomach just now for another quarrel.

"I suppose I won't," he said.

She laughed and went away to get one of the customers a drink. While she was pouring, she began to hum along with the record on the phonograph. She felt better of a sudden. The girl from the hill was gone; she hadn't found Jean. He was here, and it was going to be a long night.

A violent gust rattled the shutters.

Go ahead and blow, she told it silently. She hoped the storm lasted for days. She hoped the whole town flooded and they were trapped here in the inn. What did she care about that? She had everything she needed or wanted right here.

"You mustn't be afraid," Antoinette said. Her husband was seated on a stool in the corner of his room, huddled together despite the heat from the ample fire. "It will blow over soon."

He was afraid of storms. It was one of a long list of things of which he had always been frightened, but his fear of storms easily outreached all of the others combined. Marc had flatly refused to come along with her to look in on him, and Marc rarely ever refused to do what she wished. But he had seen his father during these storms before, and knew that he was too easily driven over the brink that separated his normally placid behavior from violence. The slightest thing—the dropping of a spoon off his tray onto the floor—might send him into a fury, and have him clawing at your throat with those surprisingly strong hands of his.

Antoinette was not afraid, not of him, nor the storm, nor of anything else. Nor of you, you foolish girl, she thought, glancing up at the photograph of Margaree taped to the wall. She felt confident that Marc's cleverness this evening had effectively brought an end to the affair between Jean and that girl. Heart-broken, the young fool would no doubt give up her dream of Stornoway, and leave, crawling back into whatever hole she had come from where she could nurse her wounds.

She would fix an annuity on the girl, though. It was a surprisingly generous thought on her part. But the truth was that, except for the rivalry between them for the house, she did not mind the girl so much. She had spunk; not enough to accomplish what she had set out to accomplish, but she was no namby-pamby at least. And there was something else about her that appealed to Antoinette's maternal instincts. She took care of her own; she took care of Marc and Berthe, and she had even taken care of Ralph, and the children. So long as they all recognized her as mistress, she did not mind the role of benevolent monarch. Once Margaree saw her supremacy, she would be generous with Margaree too. The girl was part of the family, after all. She might try to keep the Harrod name, and a Harrod could not live in a hovel like ordinary trash.

The possibility that Margaree might manage for herself did not even cross her mind. Hardly anybody managed for themselves. That was what gave the few like herself their advantage. Her strength was in the weakness of others more than in any quality of her own, and she was clever enough to see this.

She had done all that she could do to calm Yves. He would not speak, but he rarely did, and he seemed to have settled for the duration on his stool in the corner.

She was halfway back to her own room in the other wing of the house when she remembered that she had not locked the door to his apartment.

She hesitated for a moment, and then went on. It did not matter. He was hardly likely to leave his rooms tonight, with the storm blowing. She would lock it up again in the morning.

CHAPTER 18

Jean's boat still was not at the wharf. Margaree watched the boats there being tossed about like so many playthings of the waves. He could not possibly be out in this weather. It would be madness. He must have taken the boat elsewhere for the night.

There was nothing she could do but turn and start the trip back to the house. It was easier going back, despite the fact that the winds were getting worse; they were behind her now, actually seeming to push her up the hill. Her feet seemed to want to run, and she had to hold herself back to a sensible pace.

She reached the front courtyard. She did not go into the shelter of the arched door, however. She did not want to spend the night in her room in Stornoway, haunted by the thought of her foolishness.

She went through the connecting arch, across the big central courtyard. At each sheltered spot she paused to get her breath. Her limbs felt doubled in weight, and she was glad when at last she stumbled against the door of the glass house. She shoved it open; something moved from the shadows near the stables, and she saw the big dog loping toward her, looking uncommonly happy to see her.

"I can't say I blame you for wanting in," she said, letting him come into the cottage with her. "This is no night to be out adventuring."

The cottage was cold and dark. She shrugged off her slicker, throwing it across a chair in the kitchen area, and busied herself making the room a bit more comfortable. The fire had been laid, she had only to light it and the lamps, and already the place was more welcome.

A window gave a violent rattle, sounding as if it were about to yield before the pressure of the wind. She saw that the shutters weren't up, and remembered that most of the servants were away. Marc had apparently forgotten the windows here, or decided to let them go on the chance that the storm would not break them in.

She did not relish the idea of going out into the wind and rain again, but she liked less the idea of a window breaking and flinging glass all over her. She donned the slicker and went out, to the storage closet that Jean had explained held the shutters for the windows.

The heavy shutters were clumsy to handle in the

wind. She had to look at the fastening to see how they went up and then get them one at a time up to the windows, and fastened in place. It was a laborious task, fighting against the wind that tried to seize each shutter from her hands. She decided to concentrate on the window wall overlooking the ocean, and pray that the other windows, less buffetted by wind, would be all right as they were.

It seemed to take hours of arduous work to get all the shutters up. She was growing steadily more fatigued, so that it was hardly surprising when, putting up the last but one, the wind finally succeeded in snatching the wooden covering from her hand. It sent it crashing through the window, in a shower of glass. The dog, who had waited inside, began to howl.

She fought with the shutter, and managed finally to extricate it from the broken window. Better to finish with this than to stop now to survey damage.

At last she had it and the last one up. She hurried around the house and came breathlessly inside, slipping wearily out of the raincoat. The dog wagged his tail enthusiastically at sight of her and came over to tell her with looks and nudges about the shutter that had come sailing through the window.

There was not so very much damage after all. That corner of the room had glass scattered on the floor. A vase that had been sitting atop a bookcase had been toppled too and lay in several pieces.

The fire that she had lighted earlier was burning pleasantly by this time. It tempted her to forget the broken glass and sink comfortably into one of the old wing chairs before the hearth.

But the shutter that covered the broken window permitted an uncomfortable draft to blow through the room. She was tired enough to know that once she had let herself relax she would not easily rouse herself to activity again.

She found towels in the bathroom wardrobe and stuffed them into the broken spaces in the window glass. That done, and the draft for the most part cut off, she turned her attention to cleaning up broken glass. She found a broom and dustpan in the kitchen, and began to sweep up the debris.

Except for one large and one smaller piece that had broken out of its neck, the vase that had fallen over had remained mostly intact. Thinking that perhaps she might somehow be able to repair it, she picked it up from the floor. When she turned it over to look at the broken part, she saw that there was paper inside it.

When she thought of what she might have found, she nearly dropped the vase again. Something—sheets of paper—had been rolled and shoved inside the narrow neck of the vase. They had unrolled in the larger cavity of the vase's body, fitting themselves against its walls, so that they would not have been seen even if someone had looked down into that dark chamber.

She went to the big round table in the dining area, and sat down where she would have the most light. Carefully, with trembling fingers, she tightened the roll of papers, making them into a small enough cylinder that they could be removed easily from the vase.

They had been rolled long enough, and had dried out enough, that they were unrolled only with difficulty. They threatened to break in several places.

She held the roll open. It took no more than a cursory glance to tell her that she had found what she had been seeking since she had come to Stornoway. She held in her hands her grandfather's lost will. Her own name and that of her mother seemed to jump out at her from the paper.

The dog came to sit by her chair, sniffling for attention. She patted his head absent-mindedly. A multitude of thoughts crowded into her mind, some of them colliding with others. She tried to put them into some semblance of order.

First, she must put the will somewhere it would be safe for a day or two, until she could deliver it to the proper authorities. She looked about the room. It did not matter if the hiding place was perfect; no one but her had been searching for the document. No one would know that it had been found.

Because it was rolled, and she was afraid of cracking the paper by trying to flatten and fold it, she decided to leave it in that shape. This narrowed the choice of hiding places. She got up and examined the kitchen cupboards. A cannister that held a few spoonfuls of coffee seemed to offer the best possibilities. She dumped the coffee into a sack, put the will in the cannister, and returned it to the cupboard. Unless someone went looking for coffee, the document would be safe; and no one came here other than Jean.

The thought of him confirmed her in what she must do next. He must be told, if only because someone else must know, and he was the likeliest candidate. But it was more than that. She had admitted to herself that her drive to make Stornoway hers had been wrong, and had overcome her good sense.

But Stornoway was hers. It was as if Heaven itself had taken the matter under consideration, and written an end to the entire thorny problem by handing her the will, almost on a platter. There was no longer any quarrel about it. Now she could prove how little it truly mattered to her by relinquishing her claim, a claim that was now proven, to it.

Her heart sang. She forgot about the storm, forgot that she was exhausted. She must let Jean know at once. She grabbed her coat and went to the door.

But it was impossible to think of going in search for him. The storm had gotten incredibly worse. She could hardly stand in the open doorway for the pressure that tried to thrust her back inside.

There was a telephone at the inn, she had heard it ring when she had been there before. And although there was no phone here in the glass house, there was one in the library at the big house. She could certainly get that far in the storm, if she stayed to the shelter of the walls.

The big dog came to the door and whined. He seemed to be urging her not to go, to stay there with him. He rubbed against her legs and rolled his eyes up at her.

"It's all right," she told him. "I'll be back in a few minutes and then we'll both of us curl up in front of that fire for a nap."

He gave her a doubtful look, and stepped sideways back out of the way as she went out. She closed the door and started for the house.

It was laborious walking, even clinging to the wall of the stables as she did. The winds seemed to be of hurricane force now. They felt as if they could pick her up and fling her through the air with little difficulty.

She stopped in the doorway of the stables to get her breath. She found herself remembering the night she had encountered Ralph here. Poor Ralph, to have lost his life so ignominiously. At least if he had died in a storm like this it would have seemed a bit more heroic.

She had never learned what it was he had wanted to tell her that day. He had said that he had changed his mind about something. He had indicated that it was important; and certainly he had behaved as if it were secret.

A thought crept unbidden into her mind: had it been so important and so secret that it had cost him his life. Had someone else known about the intended meeting, known the reason for it and . . .

Don't be foolish, she thought. You're talking about murder.

The thought lingered. Ralph had been outside the dining room that day. He had heard her talking to Marc, had known that she was going down to the beach. Surely that was why he had gone there, to see her and tell her whatever it was he had wanted to tell her. And because she was late in coming, he had gone out in the boat, and it had sunk.

Deliberately? Had someone done something, caused a leak that would swamp it when he had gotten it away from shore? Had someone deliberately plotted his death to silence him?

The fallacy in that theory occurred to her almost at once. It had been she, not Ralph, who had planned on taking the boat out.

The idea that followed close on the heels of that one made her shrink involuntarily back into the deeper shadows of the stables.

Not Ralph, but her, whose death had been intended? It seemed too horrible to believe; but was it? She knew, and others had warned her, of Antoinette's determination to have and keep Stornoway. The woman would stop at virtually nothing to have her way.

She thought of Marc's suggestion that she take the boat out. He had even suggested a view spot a short distance up the coast—and advised her to stay out from the shore a bit.

Later, when she had come up the steps, she had found Antoinette and Marc in the courtyard, looking surprised to see her.

Had they expected her to be drowned by that time?

Something creaked in the stables. She started and peered into the thick darkness. But there was nothing there, it was only the old building bending before the winds.

She had an impulse to flee. She even moved toward the door.

But flee where? She could hardly go running out into a near hurricane. The storm had made her a prisoner here, in Stornoway.

The panic passed, and more calmly she realized that the family did not yet know of the will. They had no reason to think their cause urgent, if cause it was. It was true that if, and she could not say more than "if," they had tried once before to murder her, they might try again. But there was nothing to say that it would be tonight. Chances were that it would not; the storm would occupy their minds as well. At the very worst, she was in no greater danger than she had been in a few minutes before, or earlier in the day, or the day before. The only thing that had changed was her fear.

That, and the fact that she had found the will. And this new line of thinking made it all the more imperative that she reach Jean. No matter how angry he might be, she knew that if he thought she were in danger, he would come. She must find him, and tell him about the will. She dared not think what might happen if Antoinette somehow learned that she had found the lost will.

She made herself leave the sheltering darkness of the stables and continue on toward the house. She could not rid herself of the feeling that the house watched her approach with evil eyes. She knew that she might be walking toward danger. But if she kept her head, it should be all right. There was every reason to think that she could go into the house, make her telephone call, and come back to the glass house without ever seeing anyone. She would leave a message for Jean. Whenever he came back to town, he would be coming here, or going to the inn. In either case, soon after the storm had abated, he would be with her. She would give him the will, put herself under his protection, and there would be no further need for fear on her part.

It did seem as if things were going as she had foreseen them. She reached the house at last, dripping with rain, and feeling as if she had made a cross country hike. There was no sign of life, although the lights were burning in the halls. She did not have a watch, but she had already come to the conclusion as she struggled across the courtyard that it must be midnight or after. There was every reason in the world to think that the household was sound asleep.

The old house creaked and groaned in the force of the storm sweeping in from the ocean. Margaree was struck again by a sense of timelessness. These winds had swept the earth for centuries, since time began. Men came and went, but this very air rushing past her now stayed, wreaking over and over again the same sort of destruction, making fear and destruction eternal verities as well as truth and justice.

She went to the library, fumbling with a light there. The phone sat atop a splendid little Queen Anne desk. The service in town was still primitive. One could not dial a number direct, but had to go through an operator. She waited with barely contained impatience for the operator to come on the line.

"I want to call the inn," she said when the girl came on.

"The Golden Lamb?" the voice asked. It sounded sleepy and disinterested.

Margaree tried to sound calm and patient. "Is there more than one?" she asked.

"Not that I know of."

"Then it must be the Golden Lamb," Margaree said, a bit sharply. Time was of the essence. At any moment Marc or Antoinette or Berthe might wake up and come downstairs on some errand. For all she knew one of them was in the kitchen at this very moment having a midnight snack. She waited tensely while the phone hummed and buzzed against her ear.

It buzzed against Antoinette's ear as well. Lying in her bed listening to the mounting sounds of the storm, she had heard the faint tingling of the instrument on the night stand, that warned her someone was making a call. She had picked up the receiver automatically, to hear the sound of Margaree's voice. Her interest quickened.

It seemed to Margaree that an eternity passed before a woman's voice, loud to make itself heard over the background din, answered the telephone's summons.

"Is Jean Copley there?" Margaree asked, instinctively dropping her voice to a whisper.

"What?" Liz yelled. "You'll have to talk up, there's a lot of racket here."

Margaree raised her voice, at the same time casting an anxious glance in the direction of the great hall. At any minute she expected to see Marc framed in the doorway, watching her angrily.

"I want to talk to Jean Copley," she repeated. "Is he there?"

At the inn, Liz frowned at the receiver. She knew who it was calling; she recognized the voice now.

She glanced down the bar, to where Jean sat drinking morosely. He had been withdrawn since he came in. But time was on her side. A man needed certain things from a woman, and not only physical love. In time, he would accept the comfort that she could offer him, and then things would be as they were before.

All that she had to do was keep him with her until that right time came along.

"He isn't here," she said into the mouthpiece. She did not suffer any pangs of conscience over this lie. It was not a lie for the sake of lying. It was for a purpose, for Jean's sake, actually, although he might not accept that idea just now.

There was a long silence on the other end of the wire. Liz was about to hang up, when the woman from the big house said, "Can I leave a message for him?"

"Yes," Liz said. She listened warily. If it were something important, a family emergency, say, then of course she would have to relent. Suppose Jean's mother were sick? He would never forgive her if she failed to relay the news to him. She prayed a silent little prayer that it would be some unimportant news the girl wanted to convey.

"This is Miss Harrod, from Stornoway," Margaree said, choosing her words with care. She wanted to say enough, so that Jean would understand if he got the message, but not too much. She did not, after all, want the entire village to know what she had discovered. "If Jean comes in, would you tell him that I called to say I have found what we've been looking for."

"Is that all?" Liz asked. She smiled with relief. It wasn't important after all, and she needn't worry herself about passing the message on to Jean.

"I've found what I've been searching for, and

would he please come up to the house," Margaree added. "He'll understand."

"I've got it," Liz said. "I'll tell him. If he comes in, I mean."

She hung up the phone and went back to her work with a lighter heart. The girl wouldn't be troubling them any more tonight. And by tomorrow, who could say what the situation might be.

But she was inherently cautious, and when she went by Jean a little later, she asked him, "Did you by any chance lose something?"

"What makes you ask that?" he asked, looking over the rim of his stein.

She shrugged, and said, "Just wondered. You look sad, that's all. I thought maybe you'd been looking for something and couldn't find it."

"I found it," he said, and emptied his glass. She went to refill it.

CHAPTER 19

Antoinette waited until that barmaid had rung off. Then, slowly, she replaced her own receiver on its cradle. She sat for a moment, propped up with a mountain of pillows against the head of her great bed. On the opposite wall was a huge portrait of herself, larger than life, which she had always thought quite appropriate. It was of a young, incredibly beautiful woman who stared across time and space at her now.

There was not a moment's doubt in her mind of the meaning of that message that had been left for Jean. There was only one thing for which Margaree had been searching—Josh Harrod's second will, the one that disinherited Yves and left the estate, Stornoway and everything with it, to Julie Butler, in trust for Margaree.

Margaree had found it. It was a stroke of the worst sort of luck.

She met the eternal gaze of the woman in the painting. She knew what that Antoinette would have done. That Antoinette had determined to possess Stornoway, and she had done so. She had let nothing, and no one, stand in her way. Whatever had needed doing, she had been strong enough, or clever enough, to have done.

Antoinette got out of her bed slowly. She did not bother to hurry. She had already reasoned that time was not utterly crucial. The storm outside was to her advantage. The girl would not be going anywhere, not for the night. Even if Jean got the message, he would not try to rush up here in the storm. He would have no reason to think it urgent.

And by morning . . .

She slipped into a dressing gown, a long, pink gown with ruffles that framed her rounded chin. She let herself out into the hall and went calmly, silently along it to the door of Marc's room.

She did not trouble to knock. She opened the door and said, in a very authoritative manner, "I want you to wake up."

Even in his sleep he was responsive to her commands. His eyes opened at once. He blinked twice, and sat up. Instinct told him this was no ordinary summons, no mere nighttime whim. His mother was not a whimsical person.

He lighted a light. She came in, closing the door softly after herself.

"That girl," she said, and her voice dripped venom with the phrase, "has found the other will."

Any vestige of sleep feel away from him at once, and he was fully alert. There was no need to ask what other will she was referring to. They had discussed it often enough. He knew the full significance of the statement. A moment before he had slept as a wealthy man, heir to a vast estate. In a twinkling, he was a pauper, a "poor relative."

"What are we going to do?" he asked.

"What you tried to do before, and bungled," she said. "If she lives, she will take Stornoway away from us. She will take everything. She must have an accident, now, tonight. The storm is perfect for it. Someone always dies in these things, and no one will ever raise a question."

"How should I do it?" he asked; he had already gotten out of bed and was exchanging his pajamas for trousers and shirt. Neither of them felt any embarrassment over his temporary nudity. To her mind he might have been the little boy whose diapers she had, on infrequent occasions, changed in the past.

"Flawlessly," she said. She was furious, with Margaree for having come here and stirred up all this old trouble; with old Josh Harrod for having made the will in the first place; with Marc, because his previous attempt on Margaree's life had been bungled; most of all, she was furious with herself because she had shown weakness. She had allowed herself to think kindly thoughts of this interloper.

She had thought of settling an annuity on her. She had looked upon her as another of the family, to be protected and provided for. She did not often make such mistakes, and when she did she was furious.

Berthe turned over in her too-large bed. Too large because she slept alone in it now. When she slept at all, she thought bitterly, which was not often any more. The simple fact was, she wasn't sleeping as well as she had used to. She missed having Ralph in bed with her.

She sat up, angry with her inability to sleep. It was maddening really when you thought about it, and she did think about it a great deal. She had despised Ralph when he had been alive. She had laughed at him and mocked him and railed at him. She had kept him in misery not by accident but by design.

And now that he was gone, she missed him.

It was no use telling herself that he had only been half a man, because half a man, no matter how far short of perfection he fell, was still half a man better than nothing at all. You could not order an empty bed to satisfy your physical needs, nor to go down to the kitchen for a glass of milk when your stomach was queasy, as hers was just now, nor fetch her an aspirin if she couldn't sleep.

More than that, there had been *something* between them, however ill defined it had been. He had supplied some need in her. His very weakness had given her strength. Through him she had relieved herself of the frustration she suffered at her mother's hands.

She gave an angry snort and, kicking the covers back, got out of bed. She moved with large, unsightly movements. She went to the pull cord by the door and gave it a jerk. After she had done so, however, she remembered that the house was virtually without servants. There was only Louise, and she did not sleep where she would hear the bell.

Despite the fact that she knew this, Berthe gave the cord three or four violent tugs. Of course there was no response to her summons.

There was nothing to do but trot around on this cold floor herself, and probably catch pneumonia, to get herself something to settle her stomach.

She went to her wardrobe for a dressing gown. She wore one of Ralph's, a coarse, plaid thing that looked as right on her as it had looked wrong on him.

This was their fault, she thought, padding out into the hall. Marc and Antoinette. Every day she found fresh cause to be furious with them. She knew. They had never said, and she had never asked, but she knew that they had caused Ralph's death. It was because they had been trying to kill that stupid Margaree. Well, she didn't care about that, they could have chopped her up with axes for all she cared, but they needn't have drowned Ralph in the process. She would never forgive them for that, never.

Whenever she thought of Ralph, struggling helplessly, drunkenly in the water, she wanted to cry. He had always been afraid of the water, that was the awful thing about it. If they'd shot him, or poisoned him, or something like that. But drowning.

The poor old duck, she thought, and sniffed. Oh, they were awful. She would never forgive them. If she owned this house, she'd put them both out in the street, and good enough for them. What had either of them ever done for her, but make her life miserable. Like a couple of peacocks they were, always preening and strutting and reminding you that they were oh so beautiful.

She sniffed again as she moved along the dark hall. Ralph had always called her beautiful. No one else had ever said that she was, but he had, ever so often. She had scolded and snapped and told him he was a fool, but she loved to hear it all the same.

Now she'd never hear it again. And it was all *their* fault.

Margaree stood in the semidarkness of the library, her heart pounding.

They knew.

She had heard that telltale click on the telephone —the placing of a second receiver on its cradle, a second or two after the woman at the inn had hung up. It had rung in her ears like the tolling of a knell. Someone had been listening on an extension phone.

That meant Antoinette. And Antoinette would understand at once the meaning of the message she had left at the Golden Lamb for Jean. There was no question about that.

No question either as to how that woman would react to the news. She was not one to lie abed and contemplate a future no longer hers to control. She was the sort of person to take action.

It was the probable nature of that action that made Margaree's heart pound now until it threatened to break free of the cage of her breast.

She must not stay here. At this very moment Antoinnette must be contemplating how to deal with this threat to her security. Perhaps Marc was with her. She, Margaree, could count on no help from him. He and Berthe were too much the servants of Antoinette's strong will. And as for the household servants, some of whom might have helped her from sheer goodness, they were away. There was only Louise. That poor girl would be little help in a crisis. And as far as that went, she did not even know where Louise was sleeping for the night.

No, she would have to leave. She went out of the library, along the hall, to the front door.

But when she opened the door, she knew at once that there was no escape this way. She could hardly stand in the doorway, let alone go through it and cross through that howling fury to escape.

And if she did, what could she gain? The glass house? There were no locks on the doors there. If they came looking for her, she would be trapped there, with scarcely a place to hide.

She could never reach the village in this squall. Even if she tried, and Marc came in pursuit, he would overtake her surely.

She closed the door; even that took a great effort, pushing against the force of the wind that was trying to crowd into the hall.

I must think rationally, she told herself. She took a deep breath and willed herself calm. When she did, she saw that she was reacting blindly and foolishly. She had close at hand the instrument of her safety—the telephone she had just used a moment before. She had only to call the local constable. Even if the storm prevented him from coming, the act of calling would protect her. The family would not be so foolish as to harm her once her plight was known to the local authorities.

She nearly ran back to the library, snatching up the telephone once again. When the operator did not answer at once, she tapped the button impatiently to summon her attention.

It seemed hours before the same disinterested voice said, "Number please."

"I want the police," Margaree said in a stage whisper. Her throat was so dry she could hardly speak.

The phone clicked against her ear. The operator said nothing in reply.

"Did you understand?" Margaree asked, fighting an impulse to cry that was welling up within her. "I want the police. The local constable. Whatever you have here."

Still there was no reply, and after a moment, she realized the reason for the silence. The line had gone dead.

"Hello," she said, clicking the button again, although she knew there was no one to hear her. "Hello, hello."

She was answered by silence, the crowded, pregnant silence of a dead telephone. It seemed as if a million voices were waiting breathlessly, waiting to speak in a moment, and in the meantime the silence went on and on.

She put the receiver down and clapped her hands over her mouth because she thought she might scream against her will. She tried to tell herself that the storm had downed the lines; that she had told the operator whom she was trying to call before the line went dead, and that fact would be relayed to the police. But terror was rising up within her.

If, she thought, not wanting to face such thoughts and yet knowing that she must, *if they had somehow severed the wires to prevent her making another call out, then they had anticipated where she would be, and what she would try. And they would come looking for her here, in the library.*

She ran into the hall. It seemed to be alive with moving shadows. Her heart pounded; her breath caught in her throat. She must hide. But where?

The answer came to her in a twinkling—the unused wing of the house. It was a vast house. It would take hours to search it through and through, and they would surely start here, in the rooms they were accustomed to using. It might be morning before they had finished here—with the downstairs rooms, the bedrooms, probably even the servants quarters.

Close on the heels of these thoughts came another, very welcome one.

She was not entirely without help in the house. Somewhere in the other wing of the house was her Uncle Yves. It was a slim straw at which to grasp. She knew that he did not have his right mind. But from what Jean had told her, she thought that his insanity was a sometimes thing. If she understood correctly, he was rational most of the time, violent only rarely. If he were rational now, surely he would help her. She was blood relation. Even weak and spineless as he might be, he surely would not stand by and permit a murder to take place.

It wasn't much, but it was some source of hope. It was something to try for, at least. If she could get to him, she could try to make him understand. She must try. There was no other hope for her.

CHAPTER 20

She moved swiftly along the hall. So intent was she upon her goal that she nearly ran into the very person she was seeking to escape. She was almost to the bottom of the main stairs when a sound on them made her dart into the shadows. A moment later, Marc appeared, coming down.

She shrank back into the darkness of a doorway, watching him descend. If she had had any doubts about the danger here for her, one look at his face as he passed under the light would have ended them. The carefully composed charm behind which he usually hid his true feelings was gone. He was looking for her and there was murder in his heart. But it was not only that look of evil intent that frightened her so. There was something more. He was smiling in an eerie way. He was enjoying this, this cat-and-mouse game that was beginning now.

This was no reluctant killer, driven to a desperate act by circumstances or by his mother's domination. He hated her, and he was looking for her to murder her, and he would perform that act with relish.

Her blood ran cold. She watched as he paused at the foot of the stairs, looking around. Then he moved on catlike feet to the library. Again he paused just outside the door, listening.

When he went in, she stepped out of her shadows. But before she had reached the stairs, Antoinette's voice said from above, "Is she in there?"

She flattened herself against the wall, certain that they must hear the pounding of her heart. Marc stepped back into the hall. If he even came near, he must surely see her there, trapped against the wall, unable to move without attracting his attention.

"Not a sign of her," he said. "She's flown the coop."

After a moment, Antoinette said, "She can't have gone out. She must still be in the house. Find her."

"Where?"

"Look for her." Her voice was sharp with impatience.

Marc stood for a moment contemplating the many closed doors. He went into the drawing room, walking stealthily.

She did not wait to see any more. As soon as he had gone into that room, and out of sight, Margaree sprang from her hiding place and ran. She dared not risk these stairs, for fear Antoinette might be hiding there. She raced along the hall toward the rear of the house. If Marc came into the hall again, he would certainly see her. At any second she expected to hear him yell "Stop."

She reached the alcove at the rear, and then the room that faced the terrace. No one had yelled, or tried to grab her as she ran.

She clambered up the spiral stairs in the wall. In the darkness she stumbled and hurt her knee. There was no time to examine it. She went on, limping a little.

In the hall below, Marc was once again contemplating the many rooms about him. She could be behind any of the doors, perhaps crouching behind a sofa, or cringing in a wardrobe. It could take him the entire night to find her, if she were clever in choosing a hiding place, and he felt certain she would be. The fact that she had disappeared indicated to his mind that she was hiding. She must know they were looking for her, and why. He must suppose that and think accordingly.

He could use help in finding her, but he hadn't the heart to go back and face his mother with the deed undone, not even to ask for help. There was Berthe of course. He could browbeat her into helping with the search—maybe. She had been cool toward him since Ralph's death. He had thought at one time that she might have guessed the truth about that, but he had dismissed that idea. She wasn't bright enough to have figured that out for herself.

Well, there was one person who just might help. Who might, in fact, solve everything. He smiled wickedly as he thought of his father, driven to hysterical terror by just such storms as this one; already turned against Margaree through Antoinette's skillful manipulation of him.

If Yves were turned loose, goaded into looking for the girl, and if he once found her . . . it would solve a great many problems. There'd be no need to arrange an "accident," in the first place. He felt certain his father would take care of that for him.

At the same time it would get rid of his father. If there were a murder, the authorities would make Antoinette have him committed, and he would be out of the way. Marc did not like having him in the house; he never fully trusted that creature not to turn on him.

The more he thought about this, the better the idea seemed. Antoinette would be angry right away; but she would not have to know that it had all been planned to work out that way. He could tell her that he had simply gone there looking for Margaree, and the old man had gotten out. In time, she would get over it.

He took the stairs two at a time.

Drinking didn't help. Nothing did. Jean brushed a lock of hair back from his forehead with an impatient gesture. The noise in the room had become an uproar. The air was thick with cigarette smoke and the smell of sweating male bodies. He was a fool not to get drunk and enjoy himself as the others were doing. He had seen Liz watching him since he had come in. He knew what she wanted. He could spend the night in her bed, in her arms, and forget that Margaree had ever existed.

Well then, why couldn't he stop thinking of her? Why did the image of her face hover in the air before him? He felt sick with the pain of wanting to be with her, to have her in his arms. It was like a hunger gnawing at his insides.

It was no use. He was in love with her, and it was only a waste of time and effort trying to fight against it. He thought she was a fool to put such store on that house. He wanted to shake her and shake some sense into her pretty head, and maybe he would do just that when he saw her. It wasn't good for a woman to give herself over to greed that way. He would make her understand. He would go up to the house in the morning and talk to her. He had never really told her that he loved her, and he supposed that sort of thing mattered to a woman. All right then, he would tell her, and maybe that would help to set things right.

He gave his head a shake. So this was what love was? All that talk and singing and moonbeams, and it wasn't like that at all.

I should have stuck to fishing, he thought, and knew that he didn't really wish that.

Liz saw him get up from his stool and start toward the rear. She went toward him, hoping to coax him to go on up to her room.

Before she could reach him, though, one of the fishermen near the fireplace had clapped a hand on his shoulder.

"Did that little girl of yours find you?" the man asked. "She was in looking for you earlier."

Jean could hardly believe his ears; he stared openmouthed at the man.

"Margaree," he said. "In here? When?"

"Long time ago, seems to me. Liz, when did that girl come in looking for Jean?" He turned to Liz, who had walked up just then.

She shot him a startled look, and shrank back. But it was too late. Jean turned on her, and his handsome face was a mask of anger.

"When was she here?" he demanded. He seized Liz's wrist, jerking her toward him until their faces were only inches apart. That was what she had hoped for throughout the evening; but she had not hoped for the look in his eyes.

"Two hours ago," she said in a whisper. "About that."

"What did she say?"

She shook her head frantically. "Nothing. She was just looking for you, that was all."

He stared down into her frightened eyes. There was something more. She was holding something back. "Did she come in again?" he demanded. "There's something more. I can see it in your face, Liz. Tell me. What else?"

She was too frightened not to tell him. Trembling in his grip, she said, "She called on the phone."

He waited for her to go on. She had begun to cry, tears brimming from her eyes and running unchecked down her pink cheeks.

"She said she had found what you were looking for, and you were to come up there."

"Why didn't you tell me?" He tightened his already fierce grip on her wrist. She thought the bone would be crushed by the pressure.

"I forgot," she cried. "I didn't think it was important, and anyway I didn't want you going back out in the storm. And she wasn't alone."

"What do you mean by that?"

"There was some one else there, on the extension phone. I heard them breathe once. I'm used to listening for that because my Charles used to listen in on me all the time."

He shoved her away from him, so violently that she knocked over a bar stool and sent it crashing to the floor. He ran to the front door and struggled with the bolt.

She ran after him, grabbing the back of his shirt. "You can't go out there now," she said. "It's a regular hurricane. You'll never reach the house."

"Get away from me," he cried, swearing at her. He threw her aside. His shirt tore in her grip, exposing his bare back. The door crashed open with the force of the wind, toppling a table and some chairs, and nearly knocking him over backwards.

The lights danced wildly. Several men swore and there was the sound of breaking glass at the far end of the room as a mirror came crashing down from the wall where it had been hanging.

It took three men to get the door closed after him. "He's crazy," one of them said. "What'd he want to go out for, anyway?"

One of the others had seen that Liz was crying, and nudged the man into silence.

It was like stumbling through hell. He stood for a moment clinging to a lightpost. As he stood there an oak shutter torn from somebody's window went sailing down the street as if it were a sheet of paper.

He bent far forward, and ran across the street. He wasn't afraid of the storm. He wasn't afraid of anything, not even Lucifer himself. Margaree wanted him, and needed him, and was in danger. The fury that bent the trees almost to the ground was as nothing compared to the fury within him that drove him through that howling darkness, toward the house on the hill.

CHAPTER 21

Fate had moved in her favor. She had come through the entire length of the house without incident, moving with stealth through dark empty rooms, taking the longest route for safety's sake. No one had come in pursuit of her, no one had waited behind half-opened doors to pounce upon her.

She was in the unused wing of the house now. The halls echoed even with her stealthy footsteps, and her breathing seemed to reverberate among those empty rooms. But she had come safely to the other spiral staircase, that twisted upward to her uncle's apartments.

She moved more quickly here, less afraid of being overheard. She expected to have to knock anyway to awaken Uncle Yves. The maid who ordinarily watched over him was not in evidence, and

Margaree supposed that she was at the festival with the other servants.

The door across the stairs that sealed off this part of the house was unlocked. It opened easily at her touch, giving off a faint squeak as it moved.

At the top was a short hall, and another door, standing closed. This was Uncle Yves's apartment. No doubt he was asleep by this time. She hoped that he was lucid when he woke, enough so to understand what she had to say.

She lifted a hand to knock at the door, and on an impulse, tried the knob instead; it turned, and the door opened before her.

She was surprised to realize that the room was lighted; she ought to have noticed the light beneath the door, but her mind had been too crowded full of other thoughts to pay attention to such details.

The lamps were burning, and on the hearth a fire blazed. It was a sumptuous room, fit for the nominal master of the house. A sitting area had been arranged before the fire: a small French sofa was flanked by two elegant-looking chairs covered in damask. A low table held a silver tray from which someone had earlier eaten dinner. At the opposite end of the long, high-ceilinged room was a sleeping area, with a bed twice the size of most, canopied and draped to make it almost another room inside.

She saw all this in one sweeping glance. But her eyes came back quickly to the fire. A man was seated in the corner near it, on a wooden stool. He was all huddled together against himself, as if he were tired and cold, or very frightened. His chin had drooped forward upon his chest, but he looked up now with wide, wide eyes as she came in.

"Uncle Yves?" she said. She came farther into the room. He was not asleep then. So much the better.

He made a strangled sound far down in his throat. His eyes looked as if they would jump out of his head.

She stopped a few feet inside the door. "You are my Uncle Yves, aren't you?" she asked. "I'm Margaree. Margaree Butler Harrod. Waldo's daughter. Don't you remember? I was a baby when you last saw me."

She was speaking rapidly, hoping that his mind was clear, and that she could make these basic facts clear to him quickly, and could enlist his aid. If he would only let her stay the rest of the night here—surely no one would think to look here for her.

The man on the stool was thick bodied and round faced. Because he had spent so many years indoors, his skin was very white. He was still a relatively young man, but he looked far older than he was.

He had been watching her in motionless silence. Now, with a sudden snapping movement he jerked his head around and looked up.

She followed his glance. There on the wall was a photograph of herself.

"Why, that's my picture," she cried, astonished. "It was taken from my room. Did you . . . ?"

She never finished the question. While she was still looking at the photograph, he looked back at her, and the expression of fear on his countenance became one of loathing and violent anger. He gave a cry like a wild beast, and sprang from the stool toward her.

She screamed and tried to run from him. He caught her arm, his long fingernails raking the flesh. She twisted out of his grip, and would have escaped him; but when she turned to the door, Marc was there, blocking the way.

"So here you are," he said, looking both surprised and pleased. The corners of his mouth turned upward in a cruel leer.

Yves had frozen in place at the intrusion, looking uncertainly toward the man he did not recognize as his son. He could only think that his enemies were increasing. If Antoinette were only here. If only he weren't alone with these strangers.

"Marc," Margaree said, too terrified by the madman's attempted assault to be afraid of Marc. "He's . . . he's . . ."

"Mad?" Marc said. "Yes, as mad as a hatter. Things couldn't have worked out better for me. Thank you, my dear, for coming up here and making it all easy for me."

She saw at once what he meant, and caught her breath. "You can't mean to leave me here," she cried. But his short laugh told her that was exactly what she could expect from him.

She made a futile attempt to escape past him, but it was useless. He seized her by the shoulders.

"Here, Father dear, a present for you," he cried, and flung her back into the room, into the very arms of his father. The action jarred Yves Harrod from his frozen stance. He grabbed Margaree in his arms. Her scream of terror only seemed to add fuel to his rage.

She looked into his eyes, and it was like gazing into hell, the private hell of his tortured soul. She hardly knew that she was screaming incessantly. She was aware only of those powerful arms about her, and then his hands were at her throat, strangling the life from her. The room tilted and swooped sickeningly. Marc's insane laugh seemed to diminish.

Suddenly she was free of his arms, falling weakly to the floor, and he was staggering away from her. It was seconds before she could realize what had happened.

Berthe had come into the room. She had seen her brother moving swiftly and silently through the dark house, and had realized at once that he was up to some mischief. She had followed him, coming behind him up the stairs in time to see him fling Margaree into the arms of the madman imprisoned here.

She did not take time to reason out her actions.

She had no particular desire to help Margaree. She did not in fact much care what happened to her. But she did care that Marc seemed able to get away with anything he wanted to do, anything, even killing her Ralph. A resentment sprang up within her, overpowering her ability to reason. She acted not to help Margaree but to stop Marc.

"Blast you," she said, giving him so violent a shove that he stumbled out of her way before he quite knew what was happening. She was shorter than him, but thick and big boned; even had he had time to think, he would probably not have offered her physical resistance.

"Blast you," she said again. She ran into the room, where her father was killing Margaree and, looking about for a weapon, saw the poker lying by the fire. In an instant she had seized it and begun to rain blows down upon the beast's back and shoulders.

"Let go," she cried, pounding at him unmercifully. "Let go I tell you."

The frightened creature did let go. He cried out in pain and astonishment and fear. He was truly set upon now, literally surrounded by enemies. Where was Antoinette?

"Antoinette!" he made a shriek of her name as he tried to dodge the poker that was being wielded by the other woman. "Antoinette."

"You beast," Berthe cried, continuing to pummel him although Margaree by now was a gasping form on the floor. "You don't frighten me. You used to frighten Ralph, bless his soul. You got hold of him once like that, didn't you? Scared him to death, didn't you? Well, you don't scare me. Take that!" She brought the poker down with such force upon his arm that a bone cracked within.

The old man gave a wail of pain and terror, and bolted. He reached the door that represented freedom, and there in his path was the man. He did not know who he was, or why he was there. It was an enemy, that was all his twisted mind told him, an enemy who must be killed. Yves leaped for Marc's throat.

Marc shrieked in terror now. He was too much a coward to fight well. He went down, crashing to the floor with his father falling upon him. Marc kicked and clawed to get those hands away from his throat, hands that were strong and had the strength of hell in them. Yves was too strong for him, and his terror was greater even than Marc's own.

It was the screams that brought Antoinette. She had heard Margaree's first scream, and had understood at once what it meant. She had already taken from the drawer where it had been sitting for twenty-some years a small revolver. She had made up her mind that, if Marc failed in carrying out her orders, she would use the gun to solve the problem of Margaree.

Now, hearing the screams, she grabbed up the

gun and ran from her room, along the dark halls with the icy winds rushing over her slippered feet. Her heart was pounding. She was too old to run like this, too old for all this excitement. She had lived an orderly life all these years, a life in which everything had gone exactly as she had commanded it to go. Until Margaree came. Until that blasted girl came.

Well, she would solve the problem once and for all. She would have things the way she wanted them. She had always had them so.

Something was amiss, though. Margaree had stopped screaming—those frightened bleatings that had been music to Antoinette's ears—and it was Yves who was crying, crying her name aloud.

"Antoinette! Antoinette!" His cry was a wail, the sound of a lost and frightened child.

Then, after a moment, someone else screamed. It was a man.

"Marc," Antoinette breathed her son's name aloud as she suddenly recognized his voice. She ran faster, although her lungs threatened already to burst. Her son's voice was a rising crescendo of terror. Her labored breathing had become sobs as she thought of what was happening.

She flew up the twisting stairs, her dressing gown a cloak behind her.

"Yves," she cried. She stopped at the top of the stairs, gasping for breath. On the floor before her her husband was strangling the life from her son. Marc was barely struggling now, his hands flapping ineffectually and weakly against his father's thick shoulders. Berthe stood in the open doorway, watching the scene. A poker dangled limply from her fingers, but she made no effort to use it to save her brother.

"Yves, I want you to let him go," Antoinette commanded.

It was the first time that her husband had ever failed to obey a command of hers. But this one he scarcely heard, nor did he even recognize his wife. He was past all of that, utterly consumed with terror and the need to save himself from the enemies that threatened him.

Antoinette still held the revolver in one hand. She raised it carefully, taking aim, and pulled the trigger.

She meant to kill her husband. He would no longer be of any use to her. After this, she knew she would not be permitted to keep him here.

But she was no marksman. Marc's body stiffened; he flung his arms out as if welcoming the embrace of death as it rushed down to him. Then he went limp in his father's grasp.

Yves gave a cry that was more animal than human, and threw his son aside. He leaped to his feet. Before him were the stairs down which he could flee, and only a woman, staring with horrified eyes, remained to block his path. Something, a vague thought that wanted attention, fluttered and pecked against the closed windows of his mind, but he had no time now to examine it. He rushed toward the woman at the stairs.

Antoinette did not scream. She had never in her life given in to fear, and she would not do so now. She stood her ground in the path of her husband's mad charge, as if to defy him. She seemed to know that no one could harm her unless she willed it.

At the very moment when her husband would have seized her, clamping those iron fingers about her throat as he had done with Marc, someone else grabbed her from behind, throwing her roughly aside.

Jean stood on the last step but one, breathing laboriously, drenched to the skin. He looked not unlike a madman himself, his eyes glazed with the effort and the urgency that had driven him here through the raging storm outside, carrying him to the very heart of the storm that raged here. He stood, his shoulders heaving with the effort of his breath, and his eyes scoured the scene before him for sight of Margaree.

Yves saw those eyes dart past him, and with mad cunning he chose that moment to move. One shove was all that was needed to send this new threat tumbling backward down those stairs, to break his neck, or his back, or both.

With the instinct of a man used to wrestling with nature, Jean stepped aside. The cry of rage that had formed in Yves's throat became a final cry of horror as he missed his prize, lost his footing, and went hurtling forward down the spiral stairs.

He had a moment of terror, and felt the first blow of his head against the worn steps. He knew nothing more, although for seconds longer his body went tumbling and crashing over and over down the stairs, all the way to the last step.

CHAPTER 22

It was not yet ended though. Marc was dead, and it would have been hard to say which killed him, his father's strangling, or his mother's gunshot. Yves was dead, his neck broken in that vicious fall down the stairs; but he too had ceased living before that final moment came. He had said "Enough" to the world long before.

Jean, on the brink of exhaustion himself, was left with three women, all of whom were dazed and little more than coherent. Antoinette stood where she was, pressed against one stone wall, staring into a timeless distance. She only shook her head when Jean asked if she were all right.

Berthe was equally dazed. She had burned out all of her passion, and now she wore a petulant air, as if she expected to be scolded, and was willing to suffer when she considered an unjust punishment.

Margaree was on the floor in Yves's room, still crying softly in the wake of her terror. Her eyes snapped open when Jean touched her. She saw who it was and, with a smothered little cry, threw herself into his arms.

It was an hour or better before Jean was able to sink wearily into the softness of his bed in the glass house. It had been necessary, despite the storm that still raged, but with gradually less intensity, to bring Margaree to the glass house. She had refused to try to sleep in the big house. He had gotten her safely here, and now she was in the deep sleep of exhaustion in the other bedroom.

He had had to carry Marc's body and Yves's to their respective beds. He could do nothing more about them until morning and the end of the storm.

Both Berthe and Antoinette had declined his help in getting back to bed. Berthe had left almost immediately after his arrival, excusing herself and plodding sullenly off toward her own room.

Antoinette had looked as calm and unruffled as ever. There had been that first shocking glimpse of her, disheveled, out of breath, looking like any ordinary, frightened woman. But she had managed, within seconds, to compose herself. There was no sign of emotion upon her beautiful face. Her eyes were dry, her chin held proudly up. Wordlessly she followed Jean about in his thankless chores. She saw her husband, his head lolling grotesquely to one side, carried to his bed. She herself pulled the sheet up over him to cover his terrified face from view. She did the same for her son.

When at last a weary Jean turned to her, to ask if she was all right, she could say, with icy calm, "I want to be left alone, please."

Now she was alone. She stood before the fire in her room, gazing into the flames. She was engulfed with a burning bitterness.

She had lost. It was no use to delude herself; she had never been anything but frank with herself. Yves was dead. Marc was dead. She had seen in Berthe's eyes what had perhaps been there for years, unrecognized—a loathing for the woman whom nature had given her for a mother.

Stornoway would be taken from her; it belonged, as it actually and rightfully had all along, to Margaree. At best she could expect nothing more than a charitable invitation to stay on.

Worst of all, she had not only lost Stornoway, but she had lost it in the worst way, in disgrace and humiliation. There would have to be hearings, perhaps trials, over the deaths. The family wash would have to be aired before gawking peasants. She might even have to go to prison. At the least there would be a disgusting, tasteless uproar, a circus for the locals.

She felt sick, and the disease was a new one for her; she was suffering defeat. In her entire life, everything had bent before her will. Now her will lay shattered, and she could not even comprehend quite how it had come about. She could blame Margaree, but she could not understand what strength Margaree had had. Certainly she, Antoinette, was a stronger person, with a stronger mind.

And yet Margaree was mistress now of Stornoway and she had the taste of ashes in her mouth.

Ashes. She looked deep into the fire, as if expecting to see written upon the flames some balm for her troubled spirit. She could not pray, because she did not believe in the God of Christians. She could not believe in a God she did not respect, and she could not respect a God who would send his son to die like a thief when he could have ruled like a king. So she had thrown in her lot with the God of personal power. But he too had failed her and now it was she who faced an ignoble cross.

She would rather burn through eternity, in flames like those dancing before her now, than make a spectacle of herself and her defeat.

She knew at last what she must do.

Margaree turned fitfully on her bed in the cottage. She was haunted by dreams in which a slobbering madman chased her through the echoing halls of Stornoway. Somewhere in the distance was Jean, and she kept calling his name, but she could not find him.

The halls were lit by torches, and as she ran, their flames burned brighter and brighter, giving off an ever-increasing warmth that became an uncomfortable heat. She could hear the crackling of the burning wood, and the light danced a pattern across her closed eyelids.

Suddenly she opened her eyes, and saw that the dream was real. The room was red with the glow of fire, and the night's chill had been chased away by a thick, penetrating heat.

She sat up, crying "Jean!"

In a twinkling he was at the door, sleepy but alert. He saw that she was safe; then he too saw the light, and felt the heat.

"Stornoway," he said in a whisper, and disappeared from the doorway.

She jumped from the bed and ran after him. He was in the courtyard outside when she caught up with him. The storm had become a gentle trickle of rain stirred by a lingering wind. The rain was not enough to extinguish the flames that, encouraged by the gusting wind, were hungrily devouring the great house.

At first Margaree could hardly believe the house would burn. Her first thought was of stone walls. But at once she remembered beamed ceilings, worn wooden floors, paneled walls hung with paintings and draperies and tapestries. There was more than enough to make an inferno of the house. The heat and light and roar carried easily to the cottage. Below, in the village, someone had begun to ring the alarm bell to summon the villagers. Soon the fire volunteers would be rushing up the hill; but anyone could see that they would be too late to save the house.

Jean ran toward it, with Margaree close at his heels. But the heat was like a wall that held him back. The very stones of the courtyard seemed to be on fire.

Berthe had somehow escaped from the other side, and as Jean fought to get closer to the house, she came staggering about it. She was coughing and gasping for air, and her hair had been singed almost off, but she appeared otherwise unhurt.

"Antoinette?" he asked her, helping her away from the fire.

"She's in there," Berthe said, coughing between words. "She started it. She could have killed me. She didn't care a fig if I got burned alive."

He gave her over again to Margaree, and would have tried again to reach the house, but the heat had grown so great that flames erupted in the stables almost at their sides, and in a moment that building was an inferno too, its ancient timbers burning like paper. Men had begun to arrive from the village. They saw at once what Jean had not yet admitted to himself—Stornoway was lost, and anyone still in it. Louise, they told him, had escaped from the servants' quarters when the fire had first begun. Marc and Yves were beyond saving. As for Antoinette, one of the men had thought he saw her at the tower window, but it had been only a glimpse, and he was not certain whether it had been her, or only an illusion created by the flames and smoke. He was inclined to think it the latter, because a real woman would certainly not have stood so motionlessly calm as this one had seemed to do. He had seen fires before, and people trapped in them. They cried or screamed, those people, or jumped, even when jumping must certainly cost them their lives. But this shadow that looked like a woman had only stood and stared imperiously from the window, like a queen surveying her kingdom.

EPILOGUE

A young man stood on a cliff overlooking the sea. In the distance he saw a glimpse of white against the bluish green of the ocean. A ship was coming about the cape, toward the village below. Perhaps it was his father, who had been gone almost a week now crab fishing.

He turned toward the cottage behind him, where his mother sat in the afternoon sun doing her needlepoint.

"How rich are we?" he asked. He was referring to a conversation they had had a day or so before, in which she had admitted that fact, which he had already been told by his schoolmates.

She looked up from her work, taking a minute to consider the question. "That depends upon your viewpoint," she said, smiling. "Compared to the way I grew up, we're very rich. But as rich people go, I suppose we're really small time. What makes you ask?" She supposed there was some childish desire that prompted the question—a toy he had seen that he wanted.

"If we're so rich," he said, "why does Father have to go out fishing to make a living?"

She looked surprised by the question. "Because he chooses to," she said. "And if you want to know why, you had better wait and ask him that."

He thought for a moment, and then asked, "When I grow up, will I be a fisherman?"

"If you want to be," she said, and added, "It's an honorable job."

He seemed satisfied for the present. He left her, and went around the cottage, across the great stone courtyard on the other side, to Stornoway.

He could not say why, but he loved these crumbling walls. There was nothing but a shell of blackened stone here, with weeds growing here and there in what once had been grand rooms. He had played here from his earliest years, imagining the house as he thought it had been before it had burned, peopling it with lovely people—handsome and brave princes, and lovely young ladies in distress, fashioned more or less after those in the stories his mother used to read to him.

He climbed a shaky spiral stairs that led nowhere, ending abruptly in space. From here he could see all the way down to the village, and would see when his father started up.

He had asked once why Stornoway was allowed

to stand in ruin as she did, and his mother had replied, evasively he thought, "Because I want to be reminded," and had declined to discuss it further. His father had winked at him and said that was because she was stubborn, and didn't like to admit it when she was wrong. But that hadn't made it any clearer for him.

It was all right though, because he had subsequently learned that Stornoway was his, or at least it would be when he came of age. And he had a secret, that gave spice to his meanderings through the ghostly walls.

He meant to rebuild it. He wanted to see those walls towering to the sky as they once had towered. There would be turrets and grand stairs and fine paintings, just the way he had heard it described by some of the fishermen in town.

He did not know where it came from, this urge, but it was already in his blood. He was eager to grow, to reach manhood, so that Stornoway could be his—truly his.

Made in the USA